"So you're awake."

Startled, Theresa looked back to the door. A man gazed in at her. "Who are you?" she asked.

"Shawn. Shawn Malone." He leaned into the door frame, head ducked low to keep from bumping it on the top. "I'm the fellow who fished you out of the sea." Then it all came back to her for the second time. The commotion. The falling. The splash of water. And then that horrible dizziness on the dock, with someone holding her, talking to her.

"You? You were—"

"I'm afraid so. Whacked your head on my boat on the way down, so I felt guilty enough to fish you out. You don't mind, do you?" He laughed, pulling himself loose from the door.

She remembered that laugh and moaned, sinking back into the covers. She touched her head, felt a bandage and the dull thud of her heart pounding behind her eyes. "Tell me where I am. And what I've done. Have I embarrassed myself at all—besides falling off the dock, I mean?" She closed her eyes and turned her head away as he stood beside her bed.

Then she felt the gentle tug of his hand on her chin. "Look at me, babe," he said.

"My name is not babe," she said, gritting her teeth. "My name is Theresa."

"Terry—"

"Not Terry. Theresa!"

THETIS
ISLAND

Brenda Willoughby

Serenade/Serenata
BOOKS
of the Zondervan Publishing House
Grand Rapids, Michigan

A Note From the Author
I love to hear from my readers! You may correspond with me by writing:

    Brenda Wilbee
    1415 Lake Drive, S.E.
    Grand Rapids, MI 49506

THETIS ISLAND

Serenade/Serenata Books are published by the Zondervan Publishing House, 1415 Lake Drive, S.E., Grand Rapids, Michigan 49506

Copyright © 1986 by Brenda Wilbee

ISBN 0-310-47542-2

Edited by Jane Campbell

Printed in the United States of America

86 87 88 89 90 91 / 10 9 8 7 6 5 4 3 2 1

CHAPTER 1

A SEAGULL'S SHRIEK WOKE Theresa Parker, but the picture on the west wall was what really brought her awake.

"I can't get away from you," she whispered, her voice soft and lonely in the quiet of her first morning back at Thetis Island. She sat slowly, leaning against the pillow and wall, and rubbed the sleep from her eyes. The blankets brushed about her feet and unconsciously she pulled them around her waist to keep off the chill as she stared at the picture. Apparently it was one taken at graduation, and she felt the threat of warm tears. How come she hadn't noticed the picture last night when she'd lugged her suitcases in and plunked them on the floor? *Because I was tired*, she reminded herself and forced herself to look away.

Same old knotty pine paneling, she noted. Same old nicks and scratches. The priscilla curtains, once the color of summer sunshine, were faded and looked shabby. They were closed, blocking the view and the day. There were the usual summer things scattered about: beat-up paperbacks in a brick-and-board bookshelf; the old popsicle-stick pen holders they'd made as kids. Which one had Ron made? she wondered ruefully. Two driftwood lamps sat on the dresser; the closet spilled life preservers and boat oars out the half-opened door. The old blue broom she'd bought for Auntie Sue one summer sat in a corner. And there was that picture on the west wall. Theresa couldn't help looking at it again.

Ron Johnson was a handsome man. No other word for it. Handsome, with blue, blue eyes set far apart in a keen, intelligent face. His mouth was what all of her writer friends back in the States would call sensual, with the bottom lip full and curved, not in a pout, but in a provocative swell. Theresa could almost feel his kisses, the light touch of his lips on her skin. Then the warm tears grew hot and she had to blink quickly to keep them in.

Suddenly she threw back the covers and jumped out of bed. Yanking a suitcase from behind the door, she slung it onto a stuffed chair that seemed to crouch in the corner of the small room. Dust poofed out of the cushion and danced in the morning sunlight seeping through a crack in the priscilla curtains. She shivered, popped the suitcase clasps, and began rifling through the neatly folded shirts and shorts to find what she wanted. A bright pink blouse, blue jean cut-offs. Her sandals. Her fingers trembled with the cold as she struggled to push the buttons through the holes.

"You can't make me cry, Ron Johnson," she muttered, wiping her face with the back of her hand. *You can't. Not anymore.* But then she couldn't hold the tears, which made bright dots where they splashed onto the pink cotton.

"Oh, Ron!" she cried, falling back onto the bed, aching with loneliness. "Why did you do this to me? Why did you go off and leave me? Why?"

At last the smell of dust filled her nostrils and Theresa began to remember the tasks that had to be done if she were to be comfortable for the month and a half her aunt and uncle said she could spend here. She had to dust. Shake out the blankets. Sweep the floors. Get rid of the cobwebs. . . .

There came again the shriek of the gulls. She listened, weary from her tears. If she were still enough, she could hear the sound of the waves. And sparrows chirping. And chickadees. Other summer birds.

Quietly, methodically, Theresa finished dressing and pulled back the curtains. Without bothering to look outside, she rummaged through the closet and found enough hangers to hang her clothes. She squeezed them in with everything else. *Brush your teeth*, she said to herself, *then fix some breakfast*. She refused to look at Ron's picture as she walked out the door. When had her aunt and uncle hung it there? And why?

The bathroom was a lean-to affair, an attachment to the cabin, and daylight poked holes in places through the two-by-fours. When she was fifteen her father had built it, the summer before he had been killed. Two lives ended, her mother's and her father's, because someone had gotten intoxicated and driven their car. And not once in the eight years since had her uncle suggested finishing the bathroom. So it stayed a lean-to, studded in with tar paper and shingles and a creaky floor.

A large spider sat in the bottom of the sink. She swiped a square of toilet paper over him and dumped him into the waste can. Then, lowering her head, she unfastened the three rollers and undid the rubber band that had held her hair on top of her head for the night. Straightening, and tossing it loose, she felt her hair settle around her shoulders, layered and curled and ready to go. Peering into the cracked mirror propped up on the bathroom sink, she dabbed at her blond eyelashes with mascara. *Why do I bother?* she wondered. *Nobody out here to notice.*

There was nothing remarkable about her face. A few freckles left over from childhood, blue eyes, a straight nose, her father's smile. It was a regular face and she never gave it much thought, except that she didn't like her light eyelashes. But blond lashes generally came with blond hair, so she had to take the good with the bad. She liked her hair.

Theresa remembered the kitchen well. The turquoise formica, left over from the fifties when her uncle and father had framed the place. The pitted and stained old sink. The stubborn, antiquated hot water heater that sat in the corner, king of the "castle," with its pipes and width and dusty taps. The window with its wide sill full of seashells collected over the years, and an old milk bottle that said *Chehalis Dairy*, full of Auntie Sue's agates. She glanced quickly about the room, taking it all in, feeling the peace that this room always brought her. It was just as she remembered it growing up, visiting her aunt and uncle and cousins and Ron, their foster son, and then the summers she'd spent here as their own daughter.

Ron. There he was again. Was it a mistake to come here? "Just don't think about it," she said aloud, pulling out the old electric tea kettle from beneath the sink. She was already here. There was nothing to be done but stick it out and try to forget the rat. A can of cleanser fell over and sprinkled powder onto the blue formica. She ignored the mess and filled the kettle with water, plugged in the cord, and then wandered about the cabin, touching things, getting to know it again after so long.

How long had it been? Four years? When she was twenty they'd had a birthday party for her, and Ron had bought her a pearl necklace. Ron again . . .

She sat heavily in her uncle's chair in the living room and sighed. Here all was neat and in order. Auntie Sue must have been out here, she thought, tidying things up. The wood-burning stove was clean and a stack of driftwood had been brought in. Uncle John must have been here, too. The windows that were the east wall faced the cliff and water below—a spectacular view. Curious, she crossed the braided rug and looked down the sharp cliff where she'd fallen head over heels one summer. Uncle John thought she'd broken her neck. She ought to have. But all she'd gotten was a small scratch on the top of her head.

The cliff was still sharp. A trail that picked up at the foot of the porch steps led to the edge where it dropped away, and you had to make your way down the dug-out steps and embedded driftwood to the beach below. This morning the sun lit the crushed barnacles that lined the shore and caused the whole beach to glisten white in the light. Suddenly Theresa was glad she had come. Uncle John had been right. If there was a place where she could find solace, it was here on Thetis Island.

The water in the tea kettle bubbled, and she dashed about, trying to find a teacup with no mouse droppings or cobwebs in it. And then she had to hunt down the teabags. Where were they? In the Peak Freans tin on top of the fridge, where they always were—hard to reach for someone barely over five feet tall.

The cupboards were empty. Only some biscuits and a can of Campbell's tomato soup. She'd have to go down to the marina and get some groceries.

But now she took her tea and biscuits outside, where she could soak in the morning sun and stare out over the cliff at the beach and barnacles and tossed-up logs and darting seagulls. The tide was in and the waves lapped gently below, bringing the scent of salt and spray. The birds called to each other. The steam from her still-hot tea was lost in the breeze, and she held the china cup with both hands to savor the warmth. Goosebumps dotted her bare legs, but she felt oddly comfortable.

Funny, Canada was the only place you'd find china in a summer beach house. Her friends in the States, where she lived now, having followed Ron to Seattle where he was studying at the University of Washington, teased her about her Canadian ways. They laughed at her "Aunties" and "eh's" and her "biscuits" and "serviettes." They'd laugh this morning if they could see her drinking Red Rose out of china at the cabin.

Granted, the china was old, the gold long since washed off, but it was china nonetheless. Royal Albert. Old English Rose. She held the cup high and peered at the bottom. Old English Rose. A sense of satisfaction came over her and she smiled. Then she thought of her own china, the newer Old Country Rose pattern that Royal Albert was putting out — china she'd been collecting for when she and Ron were to be married.

Ron. He kept popping up. Could she ever be happy about anything again? Angrily Theresa sipped her tea and wondered how long it would go on — this aching for a bum like him.

Theresa had followed Ron to Seattle, where he'd studied at the University of Washington. She was now enrolled there herself as an English major, halfway through her junior year — and in fact was here now doing independent study. Meanwhile, she'd waited years for the man of her dreams to finish with medical school. He'd spent extra time specializing in psychiatry, only to drop Theresa for another woman. Younger, who hadn't put in the years, or emotional energy, or prayers.

Prayers. Theresa tossed the remainder of her tea out and it arched in a spray of droplets, caught the sun, shone briefly, and then fell to the ground. It depressed her, just to think of all the praying she had done for that man. Prayers put in for money so he could continue with his education. Prayers for her own patience as he spent evening after evening and weekend after weekend studying instead of taking her out. Prayers for "God's will," whatever that was supposed to mean. How foolish she'd been. All that praying, and what did she get for it?

"We can't get married." That's what he'd told her after all those years of waiting, and praying, and moving to Seattle, and collecting china. "It's just not God's will."

"But we've had an understanding," she protested. "Ever since I was fifteen. Ever since you came to my uncle's to live. Ever since—"

"That was years ago. We were just kids," he explained so kindly, so lovingly, yet so cold and deadly, his once soft and understanding eyes now hard and unyielding, mirroring a mind made up. "It wasn't right," he said. "Your aunt and uncle had no right to encourage us the way they did. You were just fifteen. I was only seventeen. You were vulnerable, what with the death of your folks and everything, and me, kicked around from foster home to foster home, never knowing any sort of security or love. We latched onto each other out of dependency, not out of love. No, Theresa, we don't love each other—not in the right way. Someday you'll see that, and you'll be glad I'm doing this. Someday you'll thank me."

When she'd started to cry he'd said, "It is God's will."

And then she'd found out that it was really another woman. Someone twenty-one and not twenty-four. Someone who could talk Freud and "family of origin" and schizophrenia. Someone with an education like his. Someone who hadn't sacrificed herself so he could have it all. *Someone who hadn't prayed.*

His picture stared at her where she now stood in the bedroom doorway. She pulled the covers up over the unmade bed, still looking at him. "Why did they have to go and put up your picture? That's what I want to know." She plumped the pillow. More dust, and she sneezed. *I've got a bit of cleaning to do right after I run down to the marina.*

No one locked doors on the island. Theresa skipped down the porch steps, warm now with the sun, and

14

picked her way carefully down the cliff. She wanted to go along the beach rather than the road.

The tide was receding and pools of clear seawater, caught in crevices and shallow craters of the barnacle-covered rocks, gave off the perfume of kelp and warm sun. The sea was clear in the tide pools and she peered into them, looking through the glassy mirrors into another world.

Crabs scurried from frond to frond of the algae. Barnacles peered out of their gray bone shells and mussels opened under the water and hordes of tiny creatures grew frantic with activity along the bottom of each pool.

Hermit crabs, like children lost at Stanley Park, skittered along the bottom of the pools. One came across an empty snail shell. Theresa stopped to watch him creep out from his own shell, become naked and vulnerable for only a minute, and then slip into the new and better one. It would be nice to be able to leave Ron behind like that, she thought, and find someone else. But people were not like hermit crabs, and she walked on.

Theresa came across a few purple starfish planted over the mussels where, with suction cups, they lifted the blue shells from the rocks in a way that only sledgehammers or lye could have done. The starfish vomited their stomachs beneath them from their very centers, enveloped the mussels, and devoured them.

Down close to the tide, waves licked the rocks and splashed over and into other tide pools. For a moment the glassy mirrors bubbled and churned, then became soft and clear again.

The farther south Theresa walked, the narrower the beach became, until at last she had to abandon the tide pools and rocks and edge along the thin strip of sand, strewn with old logs and the remains of logbooms. Rotted thongs and cracked fishing floats were wedged between the debris, and already flies had begun to fuss furiously along the seaweed strings left behind by the tide.

She rounded the spit and there was the marina. Sailboats and motor boats sliced through the water. It seemed busier than she remembered in years past. Excitement bubbled up inside and she hurried across the sand, caught up as always in the thrill of boats and the smell of creosote and spilled gasoline and the sound of yoo-hoos and laughter.

Her eyes quickly scanned the docks. Shielding her eyes with one hand against the rising sun, she squinted into the tangle of ropes and sails and bowsprits. A huge mast towered above the others, thick and impressive. Hand still guarding, she stepped onto the main dock and headed toward what looked like a fifty-foot sailboat. Picking her way over coiled ropes and ice chests and buckets of fresh fish, she was approaching what had to be the grandest, most elegant boat she'd ever seen.

The Sailing Bear. It swayed majestically in the small swell of the sea, its bowsprit hanging out fifteen feet in front, the end capped by a hand carved bear with an open mouth—as if to growl at the wind and devour it. The mast was at least eighteen inches thick, towering high into the sky. A double door led from the back deck into the cabin. Handcarved fish made up rails. She stood on the dock, heart pounding, awed by the sheer majesty of the ship. She was not aware of the commotion until it was too late.

Then a dog, barking and shaking water from its

coat, lunged into her and knocked her sideways. "Bear!" bellowed an angry voice, but too late. Theresa toppled off the dock and felt a sharp pain in her head. The next thing she knew she was in the water and a dog was barking and people were hollering and someone had her by the throat, holding her above the surface of the salty sea.

"What? What—" she sputtered.

"It's okay. I got you. That dumb dog."

Through splintered rays of light, she saw a man's face. Then, struck by a pain behind her eyes, she slipped into unconsciousness.

"You're not Ron . . . "

"No. I'm not."

The man looking down at her smiled, his face fuzzy in the ringing world she opened her eyes to.

She tried to sit, but someone held her back. Why couldn't she keep her eyes open? The light hurt. No, it couldn't be Ron. Not here. But where was she?

She shook her head to clear the fuzziness from her eyes, but a sharp zigzag of pain shot through her.

"Hey, there. Take it easy. I got you. The doctor's on his way. Just lie still."

Who was it trying to talk to her? She tried to open her eyes again.

And suddenly everything flooded in—the sounds, the smells, the tumble into the water. And the dog! She sat bolt upright, her eyes taking in everything and willing away the throb in the back of her head.

"Who are you?" she demanded of the man who held her. He was cradling her in his arms as if she were a child. He smiled again, his brown eyes peering anxiously into her face.

17

"Let me go. Please," she said, embarrassed and suddenly aware of people standing about. "Please. I'm all right."

"Just a petite thing, aren't you?" he said, putting a hand to her cheek and brushing away some wet strands of hair. "You can't be more than five feet tall." She winced and pulled away.

"It's a nasty blow you've got there," he added. "I'm sorry."

"I'm five-two," she whispered, terribly tired all of a sudden. Someone lay a blanket over her, and she leaned back against the stranger, closing her eyes to the world.

"Five foot two, eyes of blue. That better?" the man asked, tucking the blanket about her neck, his voice deep and resonant. Propped against his shoulder she could feel the vibrations deep inside his chest.

"Are you comfortable?" he asked again.

"I'm wet."

He laughed, a quiet, slow chuckle that warmed her inside. "Of course you're wet. You fell into the water. Remember?"

"No. I mean, you're wet. Your shoulder. I'm making your shoulder—"

He bent down to hear better. She felt his breath on her face, then felt his hand on her cheek again. She welcomed it; it stilled the dizziness. And almost without knowing it, she clutched his hand and drifted back to where it was comfortable again and where no people stood around and where Ron held her.

CHAPTER 2

"SHE SHOULD BE ABLE to be moved before too long. Once she wakes up and can let us know where she's staying."

"She can stay on my boat for a while. I don't mind."

"You can't just hold onto her, you know."

"I know that. She did keep calling for a Ron. You know any Rons on the island, Doctor?"

"Nope. Except maybe Larson's son. I'll notify the marina of her whereabouts and if anything comes up they can let you know. She should be all right. Call if she's not herself by noon, and we'll see if we can't get her shipped over to Chemainus."

"What do I do when she wakes up?"

"Find out her name and where she's staying. Then get her home and have them put her to bed."

"And if she doesn't—"

"Doesn't come around? Don't worry, son. She should be fine."

Theresa laid still, listening. One of the two voices from the next room sounded familiar, from years gone by. And where was she, anyhow?

Something wet touched her arm, and she snatched it back. Opening her eyes, senses keenly alive, she stared into the face of a huge black dog, sitting on his haunches, tongue hanging, dripping saliva onto the floor.

"Bear!" came a shout from the other room. "Where are you?" The dog picked himself up and, giving her a mournful look, trotted off. She was on a boat! Looking around, she could see that she was in a berth of some sort. Portholes let in sunlight, illuminating a small room with another berth across a narrow aisle. The wood was teak and oak.

"So you're awake."

Startled, Theresa looked back to the door when the dog had disappeared. A man gazed in at her. "Who are you?" she asked.

"Shawn. Shawn Malone." He leaned into the door frame, head ducked low to keep from bumping it on the top. "I'm the fellow who fished you out of the sea." Then it all came back to her for the second time. The dog. The commotion. The falling. The splash of water. And then that horrible dizziness on the dock, with someone holding her, talking to her.

"You? You were—"

"I'm afraid so. Whacked your head on my boat on the way down on account of my overeager dog, so I felt guilty enough to fish you out. You don't mind, do you?" He laughed, pulling himself loose from the door.

She remembered that laugh and moaned, sinking back into the covers. She touched her head, felt a bandage and the dull thud of her heart pounding behind her eyes. "Tell me where I am. And what I've done. Have I embarrassed myself at all—besides falling off the dock, I mean?" She closed her eyes and turned her head away as he stood beside her bed.

Then she felt the gentle tug of his hand on her chin. "Look at me, babe," he said.

"My name is not babe," she said, gritting her teeth. *He* used to call her that. "My name is Theresa."

"Terry—"

"Not Terry. Theresa!" she put both hands to her temples and squeezed her eyes shut. Why was she snapping at this man?

Then she realized her clothes were no longer wet and looked down at an unfamiliar yellow shirt that was big enough on her to be a dress. "What am I wearing?" she exclaimed. "And where are my clothes?"

"Sh-h-h! It's all right. You're wearing one of my T-shirts. You were all wet."

A wave of alarm swept over her. "My clothes? You took off my clothes?"

"The doctor took off your clothes," he corrected her gently.

"Miss?"

The other, somewhat familiar voice interrupted and she looked up to see a short man with a balding head and rotund face. His cheeks were ruddy and chapped and a white mustache grew thick over his top lip.

"My name is Dr. Ludlow. How are you feeling?"

"Sick. Confused. There's a pain in my head that keeps jumping around."

"Well, you've had a nasty knock-about, and a drenching besides. But you'll be all right. In fact, if you can tell us where you live I'll get you home as soon as you like. I think you'll be fine, with a little bedrest."

"My uncle's place. You know John—"

"Theresa Parker? I hardly recognize you! It's been a while!"

She didn't recognize him at all.

"You don't remember?"

"I'm afraid not."

"Seems you have a habit of knocking your head about. Your uncle hauled you in a few years back after you went sailing over—"

"Of course," she grimaced, remembering all too well now.

Dr. Ludlow laughed. "Well, it appears you have a head like a rock. You're fine. Your uncle's got that nice little package out near Smith Cove, doesn't he?"

"Yes, that's it."

"Well, let's see if we can't get you off this boat and drive you home. Your aunt and uncle there now? Say, isn't Ron tied in with you folks somehow?"

Ron? How come *he* kept popping up? "He's their foster son. But no, no one's home now. It's just me."

The doctor frowned and let out a long sigh. "When are they coming back?"

"Actually, I'm on my own for six weeks."

Dr. Ludlow pulled at his mustache and sighed again.

"She can stay with me," broke in the young man who called himself Shawn. "I'll take her home in a few hours when she's feeling better."

"Oh, that won't be necessary," Theresa protested.

"She needs someone to watch her, doesn't she, Doc?" Shawn's eyes were teasing, and she turned helplessly back to the doctor.

"It wouldn't be a bad idea," the doctor hastened to say. "You really ought to have someone keeping an eye on you, Theresa. At least for a few hours yet."

"Well then, it's all settled. She'll stay with me."

"I'm not staying with anyone. I'm perfectly capable of—"

She stopped in midsentence and pulled up the blanket self-consciously, caught in embarrassment. For the first time she saw this man who called himself Shawn Malone. Ron may have been handsome, but next to. . . .

She took her next breath of air carefully.

"Something wrong?" Shawn asked, a hint of worry in his voice.

"No. I just—" Her tongue stuck and the words died in her throat. His eyes were brown, and she remembered now seeing brown eyes through splintered light when she was being held out on the dock.

Theresa knew that she stared, and that she was being terribly impolite, but felt powerless to stop herself. Brown eyes, dark, beautiful eyes. And his lashes were black and thick, and when he smiled, as he was beginning to do right now, small lines branched out from the corners of those eyes and told her he was probably about thirty. It was as if she'd woken up in a book.

She trembled a little in his smile. It curled up at the corners, showing straight white teeth—startling white against his tanned skin. He wore a moustache trimmed short and allowed to grow just to the edges of his mouth and the curl of his lips. His hair was so dark it was almost black, and looked soft.

Get a hold of yourself, she thought. *This is not a storybook. You've had a bump on the head and you're not feeling quite right.*

23

She blinked. He was there, smiling, holding her in his gaze, and she felt a thrill of electricity skitter through her.

"I'll take her home when she's ready," Shawn said. She heard the doctor say, "Okay."

"Thank you, Doctor," she mumbled, still caught in Shawn's gaze. And then it was just the two of them and still she couldn't talk.

Brown eyes. Brown hair. Skin tanned brown. She didn't know brown could look so good.

"Well, Theresa, what are we going to do with you?" he asked. "Hungry?"

Numbly, she nodded. She remembered she hadn't had any breakfast, just tea, and that she'd been on her way to the marina to get some food and instead had gotten sidetracked looking at an absolutely marvelous boat and going for a dive in the brine.

"Yes, I'm hungry," she whispered, sensing that she was on that absolutely marvelous boat and that this incredibly handsome man called Shawn Malone was the owner.

"I'll get you something then. What do you want? Breakfast or lunch?"

"Breakfast would be fine. I haven't had any yet."

He called from the other side of the small doorway. "Shredded Wheat or Lucky Charms?"

"Lucky Charms?" She suppressed a giggle. "You eat *Lucky Charms?*"

He popped his head around the corner. "What about it?"

"I guess I'll have Lucky Charms. If you have a bowl with me," she added.

He grinned. "I had planned on it."

Allowing herself to feel a measure of contentedness, she slipped down into the warm embrace of the berth. Outside the sun was high in the sky and the seagulls perched on pilings. She could hear the clatter of bowls coming from beyond the wall, and she thought about the morning and how it had all turned so upside-down.

What would Ron think of her in a strange man's boat, tucked into his T-shirt, being served Lucky Charms? He wouldn't like it. But then, what did he have to say about it?

"I've got everything set out on the back deck. You think you're up to going outside?" Shawn squatted beside her, smiling. She had an impulse to reach up and touch his face. This was silly. She was behaving like a foolish high-school girl with a crush on the captain of the football team. And she wasn't a silly high-school girl. She was a jilted woman, twenty-four and on her own, trying to sort out life and find some sort of peace in a world that was always running away from her.

She didn't touch him. Instead she said, "Yes, I think so," and slipped out from under the covers. Then she giggled again. The yellow T-shirt came to midthigh and hung off her shoulders. "Good grief, this is huge!"

"Looks perfect as a dress. And you look great."

She knew she blushed. She could feel the steal of red heat creep up her neck and cover her cheeks.

"Now I've gone and embarrassed you," he said. And before she knew it he had picked her up and started for the door. She started to protest, until a rush of dizzy waves swooped in. He tucked her head to his shoulder and pushed through the door.

"Let me get my clothes," she pleaded.

"They're still damp. Besides, they're a little hard to reach right now."

"What do you mean?"

He carried her effortlessly and with such control. They passed into an incredibly beautiful salon with a roll-top desk and leaded glass cabinets. And was that a fireplace she saw? A fireplace on a ship? She tried to turn but Shawn mounted a few steps, flanked by railings of the same carved fish she'd seen outside the boat. Then they were outside.

Blinking in the brightness of the sun, she gasped. Flying high on the mast were her pink shirt and cut-offs, and both sandals.

"Put me down," she said sternly.

"What's the matter?" he asked, holding her firmly in his arms. "You don't like my clothesline?"

And then somehow they were both laughing and his face was close and for an instant it seemed that time stood still while she stared into his eyes. Then he blinked and the spell was broken and he set her down.

He towered above her, standing in the way of the sun's rays. She could hear her bright pink blouse flap over his head. "Good heavens!" she cried, astounded at his height. "How tall *are* you?"

"I thought you'd never ask," said Shawn Malone, grabbing hold of a line. "I'm six-six in my bare feet. And I'm very pleased to meet you, Theresa." And then he bent to kiss her, a light, quick kiss that left her breathless and just a little bit frightened.

"Tell me," he said, as if it were nothing.

"Mmm?"

"Tell me—who is Ron?"

Ron. She'd forgotten about him for a second. She looked away, out to the water and the hustle and

26

bustle of activity. A small motorboat was filling up on gas. Two men with crab nets were taking off. Another boat was tying in and children were clambering out, racing for the marina.

"Why?" she asked, still looking away, the magic of the morning gone now.

"You called for him. And I wondered."

"Well, he's nobody," she said. She said it again, a little louder this time, and tossed the wind-teased hair out of her face. "Ron is a nobody."

Shawn settled onto the locker opposite Theresa, the large oak helm between them, and spread out his long legs and leaned against the cabin. He was wearing blue jeans faded almost white and a gray sweatshirt with the sleeves torn off. As he crossed his arms over his chest, Theresa could see the swell of his biceps and remembered the easy way he'd carried her. He didn't say anything, seeming content to sit and watch her. Nervously she glanced about the small bay. The children she'd seen earlier now raced the beach, stretching their legs.

"Aren't you going to eat your breakfast?" he asked at last.

"Sure. Where is it?"

"Oh, yeah! I forgot to get it for you, didn't I?" His embarrassment made her grin. He handed her a green Tupperware bowl full of Lucky Charms. "Milk?"

She nodded. "I thought you were going to have some."

"I'd rather watch you." He settled back to his old position. She swallowed a mouthful self-consciously without bothering to say grace. He watched like a hawk. And she'd forgotten how bad this sort of cereal was. It tasted like sugared cardboard.

"Ron is an old lover, isn't he?" he said suddenly.

"No, he isn't," she denied quickly.

"What is he, then? Don't tell me he's your brother."

"No, he isn't my brother."

"Who is he, then?"

"I told you—nobody."

He shook his head slowly, a slight smile coming to his face. Thin lines came to his cheeks beside his mouth and mustache, and Theresa concentrated on the cabin door beside Shawn to avoid his face. The door hung open and she could see into the dim interior and the barely outlined form of a fireplace. Then she glanced back to Shawn's face, tanned and handsome and terribly intense.

"You don't call for people who are nobody when you're drowning," he said quietly. "You want to know what I think?"

"No."

"I think Ron was your old lover and he ditched you. And so now you're running away and trying to forget he ever existed. Am I right?"

Theresa scowled. What made this man think he knew so much?

"I am right. I can tell by your reaction."

"So what if you are?" she demanded angrily, suddenly turning her full attention to him. "Is it any business of yours, really? What right have you to go digging into my life?"

His laughter stopped her—and infuriated her. "Thanks for breakfast," she said, sitting straight. "But I had better be going, if you'll just get my clothes. Please."

"Hey, what's your hurry? Got something set up

28

with Ron?'' He grinned and sunlight played over his face. ''You know, you don't fool me a bit, Theresa. There now, sit still.''

''Let go of me, or I'll—''

''You'll what? Scream?'' He brushed her hair back from her face, holding her tight and smiling down at her. ''Are you going to holler for Ron to come and save you?''

She could feel the raw power of this man's strength, something Ron had never had. The wind ruffled Shawn's hair softly as sunlight reflected off his marble brown eyes.

Suddenly Theresa was crying and couldn't stop. The man holding her wrist so tightly suddenly let go, and she turned away, humiliated by her tears.

''Hey, there,'' he said gently. ''I didn't mean to— I'm sorry, Theresa.'' She had neither strength nor desire to resist when he slipped an arm about her shoulders and cupped the side of her face in his palm. His gentleness only made it worse. How long had it been since anyone had held her? In the back of her head she knew she really didn't want to be anywhere else.

He set his cheek over the top of her head and said nothing, simply let her cry. Then he pulled a blue bandana from his pocket. ''Thank you,'' she whispered.

A *whoof* and a wet nose startled her. She pulled loose from Shawn's arms and came eye-to-eye with the huge black dog. It was the largest, fattest black Labrador she'd ever seen.

''Meet Bear,'' said Shawn, scratching the huge dog's head. The dog backed up a bit. ''The miserable mutt responsible for knocking you into the sea.''

Bear whined, and Theresa cautiously held out her own hand.

"He won't bite," said Shawn, tugging the big dog's ears playfully. "He really is a very friendly beast. Where've you been, you miserable mutt?"

"What kind of dog is he? Not the normal run-of-the-mill Lab."

"He's not. He's a purebred Newfoundland."

Dizzy circles suddenly danced behind her eyes and Shawn's voice came to her through clouds. "Well, Bear's certainly a good name for him," she mumbled, clutching the edge of the locker for support.

"He's a good dog. Hey! What is it?"

"I'm all right. Just dizzy for a moment, is all."

"You don't look good. Maybe we should get you back to bed."

"I'm okay. Really."

"Your head still hurt?"

"No. Well, a little, maybe. But, I'm fine."

"Are you sure? You winced just now."

"I'm sure." She was touched by his concern, especially since she'd have had to moan and clutch her head with both hands before Ron noticed anything.

"It's nothing," she said again. "I think maybe I cried too much."

"You needed to get it out of you."

That was probably true. Then she realized that Bear was whining and pushing his nose into her lap, looking at her with sad, bright eyes. She rubbed his nose and Shawn jumped to his feet.

"Good grief, look at the time! It's well past noon. No wonder Bear is nosing around."

"Noon?"

"Incredible how time flies when you're having fun!" His eyes smiled at her as the dog's tail thumped the floor. "All right, all right, I'm getting it," he said to Bear.

He descended into the salon. Theresa listened to the muffled noises coming from inside while the dog waited beside her, dripping saliva onto her leg.

"There you are, Big Bear," said Shawn, dropping a large burnt bucket onto the dock. Bear scrambled up, dashing his tail vigorously. She ducked.

Shawn caught her before she hit the deck.

"Must have moved too fast," she mumbled, holding onto his upper arms, embarrassed by her weakness. But the dizziness kept on, swirling about as in a dream, and she drooped her bandaged head to his shoulder.

"Making a habit of this, aren't we?" he said, patting the back of her head softly. "There. You all right now?"

"I think so."

His eyes bore into hers and sent a shiver down her spine. She struggled to free herself. She mustn't let him know how she felt. How *did* she feel? Silly, but she'd get over it.

"I'm all right," she repeated. "I just keep getting dizzy."

"I'm going to put you down for a nap and then get you something decent to eat. I shouldn't have fed you those Lucky Charms. That marina sells groceries, doesn't it?"

"Yes, but really, I should be going home."

"Nonsense, Theresa. You can't go home as long as you keep wincing and getting dizzy."

"At home I don't have a dog to knock me around

31

and make me dizzy," she said, realizing as she spoke that she really didn't want to go home at all.

"Touché. But you're staying. You like steak? I'll get us a steak and we'll barbecue it. And I'll get some wine."

"I don't drink."

"What?" He looked down at her, dumfounded. "Don't tell me I picked a fanatic out of the water!"

"Now what's that supposed to mean?" she asked, a smile tugging at her lips.

"Don't tell me you're one of those 'born-again' freaks, one of those fanatics who don't swear, or drink, or smoke, or chew, or eat Sara Lee Banana Cake!"

"*Sara Lee Banana Cake?*"

"It's an old commercial. Came on in the sixties. Couldn't stand it." He squatted suddenly, putting his face close to hers. She took in a sharp breath. Bear crunched his food behind her. "Tell me you're not one of them."

"One of whom?" she asked, surprised by his reaction and intensity.

"Tell me you're not one of those 'born-again' Jesus freaks." His intensity shook her. His switch in mood alone was almost enough to make her dizzy again.

"I don't know," she responded carefully, feeling her way. She felt suddenly desperate not to lose this man who noticed when she winced and tucked her head to his shoulder and offered her a blue bandanna when her nose ran. She'd never denied her relationship with God before, although lately she was certainly ready to tell Him to take a hike.

"I guess that's something I'm struggling with," she said at last. It was the truth and a safe answer that would keep both God and Shawn happy.

He bit his bottom lip. "Struggling with," he said, not taking his eyes from hers. She could see her reflection in them and it made her warm and happy. Something unspoken seemed to pass, and she smiled.

He smiled back, then nodded slowly. "All right. I guess I can live with that. For now."

"Can I go with you to the marina?"

"What about your dizzy spells?"

"I'll be okay—if you leave that dog here."

"You're a hard person to turn down." He flashed her one of his smiles and the whole world smiled. *Watch it*, she told herself.

Her blouse snapped in the wind. "Guess it's time to check the laundry," Shawn said and scrambled up the mast of the beautiful boat. He seemed almost reckless as he climbed, placing his feet quickly. Then he was there, pulling her clothes loose. They fell to the deck, her sandals making two loud thuds.

"I'll give you two minutes!" he hollered down. "And if you're not ready in two minutes—"

But she had already snatched up her blouse and shorts and was on her way inside.

CHAPTER 3

THE "MARINA" WAS HALF grocery store, half restaurant. In one corner was the post office, where a tired, white-haired woman sold stamps and sorted mail. Theresa remembered her from years past. In the restaurant, red gingham curtains hung between the row of windows looking out on the docks. The curtains used to be pea green until Theresa's cousin DeAnne had come here to work the winter after she'd graduated from high school. DeAnne had studied the restaurant business in her spare time and found out that red is a better color to encourage appetites, so she'd talked Mr. McCullough into replacing the dull green broadcloth with springy red checks. It worked. Business picked up, and Mr. McCullough stayed grateful as the years passed.

"Good morning!"

Theresa turned to find the face that went with the voice and was surprised to see Mr. McCullough himself, standing at the counter behind crowded aisles of groceries.

"Well, hello, Mr. McCullough," she called out. "How are you?"

"Theresa, is that you?" The older man came around the counter, rubbing his thick, calloused hands on his apron. He looked just the same, only older, grayer, and heavier; his face was a broad beam of a smile and he came toward her quickly.

"Well, well, it *is* Theresa, and all growed up, too. My, my, what a pretty thing you turned out to be. How many years has it been, eh?" Two bright red spots rode high on his cheeks.

"Four," she said, pleased to see him. Then she remembered Shawn.

"Shawn? I'd like you to meet a friend of mine, Mr. McCullough. Mr. McCullough, this is Shawn Malone."

Shawn held out his hand, but Mr. McCullough was slow in taking it. "Yeah, pleased to meet you, I'm sure," he said. The salt and spring were gone from his voice.

"Do you already know Shawn, Mr. McCullough?" Theresa asked, sensing something wrong.

Mr. McCullough coughed and went back to his counter. "No. I've never had the pleasure." He tucked himself again behind the climbing rows of Life Savers and Cracker Jack boxes and glass jars full of all-sorts and lemon drops, and the bulk of the old-fashioned cash register. "Say, where'd you get that bandage?" His voice had returned to its normal good cheer and vitality. "You fall down the cliff again out at your uncle's place?"

"No. I fell off the dock this time," Theresa said slowly, puzzled by Mr. McCullough's sudden mood switches.

"Oh! So you're the one old Doc's been fussing about, eh? Well, if I'd 'a known it was you, lassie—"

"Shawn fished me out."

"Well, it's beholden to you I am then, Mr. Malone," said Mr. McCullough. "Theresa Parker is one of my favorites, she and all her cousins and that fine young man of hers. I be thanking you for pulling her out of the water, Mr. Malone."

"Please, it's Shawn. And you're welcome."

"And how is that lad of yours, eh?" Mr. McCullough asked, turning to Theresa, cutting Shawn short. "He finish with his doctoring school yet? The last time I seen your uncle I told him, 'You better bring that scalawag Ron up here one o' these days and let me get a good look at him.' But I been waiting still, and not seen hide nor hair of any of you folk, eh? My, my, but what a surprise to see you walkin' in here the way you did, all set for summer, with a bandage the size of a pocket on your head.

"Say, what can I do for you?" he asked suddenly. "You need groceries or a good bite to eat? That cousin 'a yours, now there's a good girl, eh? That cousin, she got the menus all fixed up so's even those Americans from Seattle give me compliments on the fixin's. What'll it be, now?"

Shawn cut in. "I think we'll just get some groceries this time, Mr.—"

"McCullough."

"McCullough. Theresa's had a pretty nasty bump on the head and the doctor says for her to be taking it easy."

Mr. McCullough fixed his eyes on Theresa. "Where's your aunt and uncle?" he demanded. He leaned over the counter, waiting.

"Vancouver. I'm here alone for six weeks. Sort of holidaying it by myself." For something to do she inspected the crowded boxes and the new paper bags of juice and milk that Canada was using to package certain products in. She picked up a paper bag of orange juice and looked at the French on the back.

"You married yet?" Mr. McCullough asked.

She was conscious of Shawn's eyes upon her. They seemed to tease, daring her to say what a nobody Ron was. "Not yet."

"And so you're staying out at your uncle's all by yourself, is that it, eh?"

"That's what I said." Theresa hadn't remembered Mr. McCullough to be so nosey before. And she knew she was beginning to sound a little rude herself.

Mr. McCullough laced his fingers over his belly and stood back on his heels. Jars of Comtrex and Dristan stood at attention over his head, lined up like little rotund soldiers on the march against allergy. "So when are you going to get married?"

That was it. The words were out of her mouth before she could stop them. "Mr. McCullough, when did you get so nosy?"

His erupting laughter startled her even more than her question. She smiled when he said, "Eh? You're right, little lassie. I been giving you a drilling. It's just that I look upon you as my own and you got me worried there a spell. But I see you got your same old spit. There ain't to be anyone that takes the best of you, eh?" He looked significantly at Shawn.

"I guess I can take care of myself."

"Well, you take it easy, lassie. This island ain't the safe place we used to be. Not with all these Americans coming up the way they do." He paused long

37

enough to let the remark set in. It made Theresa feel defensive again. The remark was clearly directed toward Shawn.

"You forget I live in the States now, Mr. McCullough," she said. "Have for nearly four years." *Ever since I followed Ron down there.*

"I'm going to let you two chat, while I get the groceries," interrupted Shawn. "What was it going to be tonight, babe? Steak?"

"I told you what my name was," she hissed, dropping the orange juice bag onto the shelf. Out of the corner of her eye she could see the old eyebrows push high on the proprietor's forehead.

"Steak it is then, babe," he said. "Excuse me, Mr.—"

"McCullough."

Theresa watched Shawn disappear between the crowded rows. Only his head was visible, towering in full view over the tops of the shelves. "My name is Theresa," she said loudly.

"So he calls you *babe*, does he?" she heard behind her. She whirled around.

"Mr. McCullough," she said, pouncing on him with her frustrations, "whatever is the matter with you? You're being rude to a friend of mine—"

He didn't blink. "You're the one who's hollering at him."

"I just met the man this morning. His dog knocked me overboard. I hit my head on his boat. What else could he do but fish me out?"

Wrinkles crinkled out of the corners of Mr. McCullough's small blue eyes and spread to his ears. "I guess he could have fished you out, said *Good day* and left, eh?"

"I told you, I knocked my head on his boat. Mr. McCullough, you don't like him, do you?"

His eyes narrowed suddenly and he leaned forward, his small blue eyes focused on her. "You're darn right. I *don't* like him." He glanced about the store and lowered his voice. "I suggest to you to be careful. He's an American, you know."

"Oh, for heaven's sake." She almost laughed. "You can't hold it against a man just because he was born on the wrong side of the border."

"He's one of those *rich* Americans, Theresa."

"Don't be silly, Mr. McCullough."

"I can see he's already got *you* dazzled. Picking you up and stowing you away on that great big boat of his. Dazzled you right into his hand, he has."

"Now you really *are* being silly. There isn't a lick of truth in what you say."

"Is that what you think?" Then he looked up. Shh! Here he comes. Hey, you like a bag of all-sorts thrown in?"

It was a game they had played when she was younger. "Your treat, Mr. McCullough?"

"My treat."

"Two then, Mr. McCullough."

"I was right!" said Shawn the minute they got outside. "Ron *is* your ex-lover!"

"Oh, be quiet."

"My, my, getting a little sour, *eh?*" He emphasized the Canadian *eh* and dropped from the porch of McCullough's Marina, jumping easily, though he held two grocery bags in his arms. Theresa noticed he didn't have to poke his nose over the tops as she would have.

"I think maybe I'll go on home," she said.

"Now?"

"I think so."

"Don't be a spoil sport."

"I'm not being a spoil sport. I'm just tired."

"You're doing fine. You haven't been getting dizzy, have you?"

"No, but my head hurts."

"Got any aspirin at your place?"

She didn't. The tops of the celery stalks and a box of crackers rested against Shawn's chest. His gray sweatshirt was caught up under one of the bags and she could see tanned skin and a tight stomach.

"Well?" he wanted to know, grinning at her now. A breeze mussed his near-black hair. A dimple popped into his cheek. Why hadn't she noticed that before? His eyes were even darker in the sun, shaded by his dark lashes.

"Giving in, aren't you?" he teased then nodded at a high-school student passing them with a fishing pail and rod. "Aren't you?"

"Maybe I better go home," she repeated.

She didn't really want to. Having barbecued steak with Shawn and spending the rest of the afternoon with him sounded so much better than dusting, shaking the blankets, and going after spiders.

"Hey, there!"

"Huh?"

"You all right? You're off in outer space again. Come on, let me fix you something to eat, then I'll take you home."

This is why I like this guy, she thought, following after him. *The way he takes control, and yet not really.*

"Say, did that Ron of yours ever tell you how beautiful you are?" he said suddenly.

That surprised her—so out of the blue, so really very untrue.

"Did he?"

"No. . . . " she replied frankly.

He blocked the way, then stooped so their faces came close and she felt a shiver of silent warmth.

"You are, you know. You are *incredibly* beautiful."

The warmth inside grew hot and she felt a flutter of excitement that told her she had better backtrack, fast. But she didn't. She just stood there, looking into his wonderful marble brown eyes.

"Thank you," she whispered.

"Well, you're welcome. And you *are* beautiful. And that Ron of yours was a turkey."

As they approached the dock, Bear loped out to meet them, yapping and jumping, and sniffed for the fresh meat at the bottom of one of Shawn's bags. She drew a sigh of relief and took her place behind them, away from Shawn's eyes and Bear's tail.

She turned to putty when he looked at her like that, she realized, keeping pace. She didn't know if she liked it. Or maybe the problem was, she did.

"Nice friend you have there in the marina," Shawn said as he climbed aboard his boat, shooing his dog out of the way. He put one bag down, took her hand, and hollered at Bear to move. "How do you say in Canada? Chummy? Nice chummy fellow. Hey, you up to getting that lighter bag and bringing it down here?"

Actually, she was feeling pretty good. Maybe it was the compliments, or the company, or maybe just the thought of having something other than Lucky Charms in her stomach soon.

"Sure!" she said. Then, "Don't let it bother you. Mr. McCullough doesn't like Yankees, that's all." She dismissed the growing attraction she felt for him. It was silly, really. He just looked good because Ron had passed her by. *Ron.* Even yet she was thinking of him.

"Yankees? You mean Yankees as in Confederates?" He laughed.

"Yankee as in American."

"He doesn't like *Americans?*"

"No. But a lot of old-timers don't. My grandfather used to own a grocery chain in Vancouver and he always advertised, 'Canadian owned, Canadian sold.' People shopped there for no other reason than that."

Bear followed them down the companionway into the salon. This time Theresa stopped to get a good look at the small room while Shawn went on into the kitchen. She set her bag on the old roll-top desk that sat on the port side of the ship. Leaded glass wine cupboards flanked either side.

"The Canadians can get pretty sick of American enterprise," she continued. "We've got Safeways and Luckys and all the major American chains up here. The Canadians feel smothered by the American dollar. Where's your aspirin?"

"I notice they don't argue when it comes to our spending it! Down, Bear! You say your grandfather owned a grocery chain in Vancouver?"

"Yeah, Wilbee's. Fourteen of them, I think. He used to do crazy things like paint footprints on the sidewalks that led into his stores."

"Sounds like a neat guy. Is he still around?"

42

"No." Grandpa was another person in her life God had let die. Lymph cancer, too. It had been horrible. She put him out of her mind.

The fireplace sat opposite the door. Blue Dutch tiles lined the wall above it, the center four being a likeness of *The Sailing Bear* itself. It truly was a magnificent ship, and for the first time Theresa wondered how it was Shawn could afford something so elegant. Was he spending an inheritance? Was he a self-made millionaire? Or what was he? And what was he doing in Canada? Thetis Island in particular?

The questions bombarded her head, and feeling faint all of a sudden, she lowered herself into the plush, red velvet chesterfield that lined the leeward side of the boat. Cool air wafted through the open door and she closed her eyes, feeling it on her face. Seagulls called outside. But the questions kept coming.

How was it she was even here? Was it really just a few hours ago she'd been crying about Ron? And who was this Shawn, this powerful, attractive man that was making her forget Ron too fast?

She must have fallen asleep because when she awoke the air was chilly and a heavy Hudson Bay blanket covered her. She sat with a start, then sank back into the chesterfield. Shawn was bent over the desk, totally engrossed in what he was writing. A fire snapped and crackled in the fireplace and she stared at the flames a full minute before putting it all together.

"Shawn?" she said, feeling a dryness in her throat. "Shawn?"

"What? Oh!" He dropped his pen. "You feeling all right?" The soft light in the salon made his face warm, his smile tender.

"I'm thirsty."

He got her a glass of water and helped her sit up, then tucked the blanket in tight. "I must have fallen asleep," she said, holding back a yawn.

"Went out like a light. I came out to give you the aspirin and there you were, snoring up a storm."

"I was not snoring. I do not snore."

He chuckled, low and full of fun. "You've been sleeping all afternoon. Hungry? The steaks are ready to broil."

"What time is it?"

"Nearly eight."

"Eight? I've got to get home!"

He smiled and tucked a strand of hair behind her ear. His fingers lingered over the bandage stuck to her head and she felt again that warm sliver of electricity.

"I told you—you slept all afternoon," he said. "And you can't go anywhere. You have to eat."

She pulled his hand away. His touch fuzzed her thinking, and she needed to keep a clear head.

"Have I told you already that you're beautiful?" he asked, shaking her hand loose from his so that he could reach for her face again. He ran his fingers along her jaw line and the shivers danced down her back.

"Yes, you did," she said carefully, waiting. He was going to kiss her. She knew it. What was she going to do?

But he didn't kiss her. Instead he said, "Are you ready for dinner?"

She nodded, surprised at her disappointment. "Yes, let's eat. I'm starved."

They sat on the back deck and watched the sun go down. He lent her a sweatshirt that dragged about her knees, but it was warm. Inside they could see the fire still crackling in its cage. Outside they could see the gold light over the water, the last of the sun winking goodnight. They fed their meat scraps to Bear, who gulped them down, and listened together to the night sounds over the water. It was peaceful and Theresa felt herself relaxing.

"I could get used to this," she said, stretching and settling back down in her chair, bundling up in the sweatshirt. "This is nice."

"Takes the pressure off of life, sitting here, doesn't it?"

"Yes. Makes you forget the world and all its problems."

"And there's a whole world out there I'd like to forget." He seemed to watch her. "Come here," he said.

"What?"

He patted his lap. "Come here."

"You want me on your *lap?*"

"Please? It was kind of nice the last time." he smiled.

She hesitated, but his eyes drew her to him and she moved like a cat across the deck—why, she didn't know.

He tucked her close, but when he kissed her it was on the top of her head. "Are you really only five-two?" he asked, murmuring in her ear.

"Yes. How did you know?" It felt so good to have someone to hold her, to ask silly questions.

"You told me. This morning."

"I don't remember. What else did I say?"

His voice was deep and low, strong in the growing dark. "You said you loved me."

"*I did not,*" she murmured back, amused with his

teasing, wondering how something so wonderful could have happened so fast. She wondered what was going on in her head to be sitting here like this. Maybe she *was* dazzled as Mr. McCullough had said.

A motorboat hummed in the distance and they listened to it draw closer. He rubbed her back, sliding his hand up and down, and they watched the boat cut its power and idle up to a dock on the far side. There was a muffled call of voices, the clank of buckets and gas cans. She snuggled down in his arms. Mr. McCullough was right. She *was* getting dazzled.

Shawn kissed the top of her head again and when she lifted her face to his, she saw that his eyes were intense, his mouth a tight line. The stars blinked on over his head, then he lowered his face to hers.

His kiss was soft, very tender. His lips were warm and at first he kissed her eyes, then the bridge of her nose. "Shawn," she began to protest. Then his mouth found hers and she didn't care. She felt the surge of his passion and kissed him back, longing for it to go on.

"You're so beautiful," he whispered, kissing her again. "You're so tiny. I just want to take care of you."

"Wait. Shawn." She struggled to sit.

"Mm-m?"

"Please," she said, pulling her arms free.

"What's the matter? You don't like getting kissed?"

"I do. It's just that—" Just that what? She didn't know. It was just too soon, too fast.

"Just that what?" he demanded, letting her go so suddenly that she lurched backward into the cold lockers. His face was hard, and his eyes bore into hers harshly. The teasing was gone, the tenderness. "Is this some kind of a game? Because if it is, I don't like it."

"That's not fair," she said quietly. "I need some time. I need—"

"I should have known. It's Ron, isn't it?"

Theresa scrambled away from him. "It's got nothing to do with Ron. It's just that—" She didn't know. "It's just that—"

"Just that what? If it's not Ron, what is it? Oh, don't tell me! It's the old 'born-again' syndrome. You're one of those Jesus freaks who don't kiss on the first date. You're—"

"I didn't know this was a date!" she cried, appalled at the words that were being flung. "And I'm not a Jesus freak."

"Sure you are. I should never have fished you out of the water. I should have just let you find your way to heaven!"

His words were cruel and harsh. She could hardly believe her ears. Ron would *never* have said a thing like that. She stepped up onto the dock, to get away from him and his vile words. The boards of the pier were uneven and she stumbled, but regained her footing, and when she got to the road she started to run.

Night owls yoo-hooed in the quiet. A snake slithered in the grass. Weary from fighting off another headache, Theresa came at last to the cabin.

She opened the back door, reached inside, and found the switch. Electric light flooded the kitchen and immediately moths fluttered about the bulb. It seemed an eternity since she had been here last, but it had only been this morning since she'd been crying about Ron and had squashed a spider. Now she was crying about Shawn and staring at moths battering themselves senselessly.

In the bedroom she slid into an old orange flannel nightie that had a scarecrow on it and the words, *If Only I Had A Brain* . . . It was left over from ages ago, but was still nice for those damp nights at the beach. She climbed into bed without bothering to brush her teeth or wash her face, or curl her hair. Or say her prayers. Head against the pillow, biting her bottom lip, arms over the top of the blanket, she stared into the dark. Moonlight cast funny grays about the room and her eyes darted back and forth, looking into the shadows. Then her gaze met with the picture.

Ron.

She hesitated, then jumped out of bed and darted across the cold floor. Grabbing the picture with both hands she scrambled back over the bed, tripped on Shawn's sweatshirt, the one she'd discarded only moments before and thrown to the floor, picked it up, and threw them both out the back door. She heard a thump and then the splintering of the glass as the picture hit a rock or stump. But it brought no comfort. She collapsed into bed and fell into an exhausted and fitful sleep.

CHAPTER 4

THE SOUND OF SOMEONE whistling invaded Theresa's sleep. At first it was only a sound in her dreams, but the dreams faded and the noise kept on. Too groggy to figure it out, she drifted in and out until the black realization that someone was in the cabin jolted her upright. She sat in the heap of bedclothes, heart pounding. Other sounds came to her ear now—the clatter of dishes, footsteps, the banging of a cupboard. There was the smell of bacon. *Someone was in her kitchen!*

It wasn't exactly fear that came to her. Whoever it was could mean no harm, or the harm would already have been done. The feeling was like the edge of fear.

She crept slowly from the bed, cautious to make no creak against the cold floor or squeak of a dresser drawer. She slipped on the shorts she'd discarded last night and tugged on a pale blue T-shirt with *Candice's* spelled in pink on it, then tiptoed stealthily toward the closed door.

Funny, she couldn't remember closing the door. There was no knob, just a wooden handle to grasp and pull. It was smooth in her palm and she stood quietly, listening, until her palms grew sweaty.

Whoever it was was whistling "If a body meets a body, coming through the rye." Still she waited, her own body cold and stiff, ready. Ready for what?

Water rushed from the kitchen tap and she tugged on the door so that it opened a crack. She could see the end of the counter, part of the window, the milk bottle filled with rocks. And then Shawn stepped into view.

"Good heavens!" she exploded, yanking open the door. "Just what do you think you're doing?" She ignored the piercing pain behind her eyes.

Shawn whirled, frying pan in hand, smile on his face. The smile froze when he saw her.

"I asked you a question," she said, feeling that edge of fear give way to anger, and the sharp stab of pain to a dull throb.

His dimples flashed. "Why don't you go brush your hair?"

Who did this man think he was, barging into her house, then telling her to go brush her hair? "You've got your nerve! You come sneaking into my house, help yourself to—"

"Breakfast?" he said, grinning again. In the morning sunlight his cheeks appeared more angular than she remembered. It suited him, and she felt the flutter of excitement deep down in her stomach despite her surprise and anger. In a rush she recalled their kisses and the warmth of a blush burned hot on her cheeks.

She looked away self-consciously and saw the countertop cluttered with broken eggshells, an open package of bacon, a hunk of what looked like Monterey Jack.

"Where did this stuff come from?" she asked, embarrassed and helplessly aware that she was in a dither.

He turned his back, giving her an unexpected chance to take a deep breath and get back on track in her head. He set the frying pan on the stove. "Go brush your hair," he repeated.

"My hair? What's wrong with my hair?"

"It's a mess."

The closest thing to throw was a pencil and she was tempted. Of course it was a mess. Everything else was a mess, too—this kitchen, her life, everything! She didn't have to put up with this.

Marching across the floor, pencil clutched tight in her fist, she flung open the back door and glared at his broad shoulders, narrow hips, and neat waist. "Get out of my house," she said.

"Well, that's a nice welcome. After all I did for you yesterday."

Yesterday. Steak at sunset and then harsh, angry words. It all came to her like a dump truck spilling its gravel in her very own kitchen.

"You didn't do anything for me yesterday," she said coldly.

Shawn turned up the gas. Flames leaped in a blue-white ring under the element.

"I fished you out of the water for starters."

"I didn't ask your dog to knock me in!"

"And all I did for you today."

"Today? All you've done for me today is tell me my hair is a mess. I could have told you that." The pain in her head throbbed mercilessly now, a steady roar

51

between her ears, despite the early morning breeze coming in through the door, chilly and fresh. Goosebumps crawled over her arms and legs. "Not to say anything of sneaking into my house and making yourself at home."

There was still no aspirin. The thought of it made the headache even worse.

Shawn dumped chopped-up pieces of cheese into the frying pan and stirred them into the eggs. "All right, I'm sorry. I guess I should have started with that. I really am, Theresa. I'm here to apologize. I was rushing things, and I'm sorry for the things I said. It was uncalled for and there was no excuse for it. In fact, I've been up all night thinking of ways to beg your pardon. That is the way you say it in Canada, isn't it? I beg your pardon?"

It was a nice little speech.

"Will you forgive me?" he asked.

He had been rude and demanding. He had been obnoxious and terrible. So why was she trying not to smile? Why was all the anger leaking out?

He grinned. "You're trying hard to forgive me, aren't you? Hey, I even cleaned up after you."

"You what?" she said, tapping her fingers on the counter and looking around. "It looks a whole lot worse than I remember it."

"Look outside, Theresa."

His sweatshirt, still with brush and dirt stuck to it, hung over the back rail, but it was the picture she saw first. Its shattered frame was propped against a post. Ron's face was looking at her now from behind cracked glass and a twisted frame, and she took a deep breath. *Really*. This was too much.

"Well?"

"Well what?" she said, biting the insides of her cheeks, one hand on the doorknob, her weight on one foot. The bacon sizzled and curled. Shawn turned each piece with a fork.

"Actually," he said, keeping busy at the stove, not turning around, but speaking to the eggs and bacon and the tin salt shaker that sat at the back of the stove, "you're lucky I even bothered to pick them up—after nearly getting hit with them last night."

She could only stare at the man she'd met just the day before. Six-six. His head only cleared the low ceiling by a few inches. He probably had to duck to get in. Finally she said, "So you spent the night here, I take it?"

"The couch was cozy. Or is it called a chesterfield up here, *eh?*" Now he turned around and rubbed the side of his face with one hand. "Borrowed your uncle's razor. Hope he doesn't mind."

"I don't think I like you."

He double-checked the stove, fiddled with the bacon. "Got any paper towels?"

"No."

"We made a deal yesterday. Come on. Sit down. Breakfast is ready."

"What are you talking about?"

"We made a deal that after our dinner I would take you home. Remember?" He spoke to her as if she were a child. "Remember?"

"Yes, I remember."

"Come on. Sit down. Here." And he pulled out a chair at the little table shoved in close to the hot water heater. He set a plate of bacon and scrambled eggs on the table. Toast with some marmalade was already set out, along with the two glasses of orange juice. "So that's what I did." He sat down and spread his napkin over his lap. "I saw you safely home. A promise is a promise. Only I hadn't counted on nearly getting hit over the head with a flying shirt and a picture frame. Come on. Your eggs will get cold. Especially with that door open."

"You followed me home?"

"I told you. We had a deal. And I'm a man of my word. I promised. Besides, I was worried about you. You know, the bump on your head and all."

"So where did"—she waved a hand about the room—"all this come from?"

"Sit down and I'll tell you. No, first shut the door. Then brush your hair. Then sit down."

She wasn't going to shut the door, but she would go into the bathroom. Not to brush her hair—as if she'd do *anything* just because he told her to—but to get away from him a minute so she could think.

That charm of his, the powerful whatever-it-was, was working overtime, trying to dazzle her. She sat on the toilet, lid down, as if it were a chair, then set her chin in her hands. He'd been harsh with her last night when she was afraid he was moving too fast. He'd followed her home and had seen her throw out the shirt and picture. He'd sneaked in here when she was asleep. And she was supposed to forgive it all because he'd made a mess of her kitchen and fixed her breakfast.

"Hurry up in there! The eggs, remember? They're getting cold!"

She got up reluctantly, took a quick peek in the mirror, and gasped.

She *was* a mess!

Her hair hung limp and choppy. Her eyes were

swollen, probably from crying so much. Mascara was smudged under her blond lashes and a crease where her cheek had lain against the pillowcase still marked her face. What was worse, the bandage had come off during the night and the ghastly gash on her head was a mess. She groaned. How could she face him? Suddenly it mattered very much that she looked nice.

"You all right in there?"

"Yes, I'm all right," she said, turning on the cold water and dashing it over her face. She winced when the water touched her bruised forehead.

"You stuck in there or something?"

"No!" She took a comb off the sink and ran it through her hair. She splashed more of the cold water on her face, gently rubbed the mess on her head with a towel, then redid her mascara.

She combed her hair again. No good. There was no concealing the yucky mess on her head, which stuck out like a sore thumb. She tried bangs. Still no good.

"Then come on!"

"Oh, darn," she cried, jabbing at her hair and somehow stabbing her head. Fresh blood oozed out of the half formed scab. And then he knocked and she froze.

"You sure you're all right in there?"

"Of course I'm all right!"

She noticed a saw hanging on the back of the door, behind her uncle's old blue bathrobe. What a place to hang a saw! She *had* to rejoin Shawn. She couldn't stay in here all day. She yanked the door open, head held high, pushed past him, ugly past gorgeous, and sat down at the kitchen table.

"Hurry up," she called. "Your eggs are getting cold."

"You know what?" Theresa said, sitting across from the nervy, audacious man. "Mr. McCullough was right about one thing."

"What's that?"

"That it isn't safe anymore to leave your doors unlocked around here. The Americans, you know."

Shawn's laugh just popped out of him, which made her smile in spite of feeling unattractive. She loved the way he laughed. But when she bent her head, resolved this time to say grace, she sensed something wrong.

"What was all that about?" he asked when she looked up.

"What?"

"I thought you said you weren't a fanatic."

Last night's words drove in. Tentatively she took a bite of egg. They were cold. She should have shut the door.

"Are you referring to my saying grace?" she asked, not sure she wanted to get into this. It felt suddenly they were worlds apart.

He took a gulp of the juice and she did, too. "Hey, what *is* this stuff?" she demanded, swallowing hard.

"Orange juice."

"It can't be. Must be one of those cheap imitations. What is it, anyway?"

"You criticizing my orange juice?"

"It's not orange juice. It's pure chemicals with a little dust thrown in to make you think you're getting pulp. How did all these groceries get here, anyway? Did you go out early this morning and get them? And what time is it?" Without waiting for an answer, she turned around in her chair to see the clock. 11:30. It was late.

"I brought them out last night."

"Last night?"

"Brought them with me. I heard you say you needed groceries. Say, are you feeling all right?"

"You didn't bring any aspirin with that stuff, did you?"

"It's in the bag."

"You're kidding! You really brought me some?"

"Sure. Here, I'll get it for you."

This was not the same man who had raged at her last night.

"Thank you," she whispered, putting three onto her tongue.

"You're welcome."

Then she decided to take her life in her hands. She might as well face the subject, instead of continuing to wonder. "Shawn, why is it you hate fanatics so much?"

He took another bite of toast in lieu of responding.

"You seem to have a real hangup about it," she went on, spreading the marmalade. Where was the lemon cheese?

Shawn ate slowly, and she watched him chew on cold toast and jam. He concentrated on the windows, looking through the kitchen to the living room and out to the water.

Finally he tipped his chair back, propped his head against the water heater and folded his arms behind his neck. Still not looking at her, but staring out to the receding tide and the arbutus trees and the sky, he said, "I don't have much use for God. I don't like the company He keeps."

That was blunt enough, but nothing new. She didn't like some of the company He kept, either. There were some real doozies, you ran into them all the time. But God loved them, and you couldn't hold that against Him! She gathered up the dishes and began puttering about, filling the sink, wiping down the counters, scraping the frying pans.

"He likes to hang around with real jerks," Shawn was saying. "You know the types. Standing on the corner in their polyesters and tennis shoes, handing out cheap tracts."

"Oh, for heaven's sake, Shawn," she exclaimed. "Not everybody's like that. *I'm* not like that!"

"I don't like how He treats His company, either."

It was as if he'd just kicked open a door. "You know," she said, pausing a moment, "I was kind of coming to that conclusion myself. He *doesn't* seem to treat some people very well, does He? Sometimes I'm not sure I like the way He's been treating *me*."

"Why? Because Lover Boy dumped you?"

The door slammed in her face. "What do you know about it?" she flared. "Life seems to treat you just dandy! With that fancy boat of yours—"

"I'm sorry, Theresa. That was unfair. Please forgive me."

"You don't know anything about my life," she said and began to clean the grease splatters off the stove. "You don't know *anything* about it."

He startled her by taking her shoulders and turning her around. He took the cloth from her hand and began to wipe the crumbs off the table. She could only stare at him.

"Let me guess," he said, scooping the crumbs into his hand. He looked around for a garbage can and she pointed to the corner. "Let me guess about your life. You were born and raised in the church, always did your homework, and before you went to bed, said your prayers. A regular little goody-two-shoes. Am I right?"

His eyes danced with fun. He was teasing her, and the mood of the room changed like a new batch of kids on a merry-go-round. "Where do I put this?" he asked, holding out the cloth.

"On the stove handle."

He slipped the cloth neatly between the oven door and the chrome bar. "I'll bet you even taught Sunday school," he said, laughing.

"More than that. I used to be a missionary."

"Good Lord!" He slapped his head and slumped out the back door. "Mind if I rest on your back step while you fill in the rest? This is even worse than I had imagined." He patted the step beside him. "Sit here and tell me exactly what it is I've fished out of the water. I hate to hear! Not only a fanatic, but an honest-to-goodness missionary! How *do* I get myself into these things?"

"I'm not about to sit down next to you," she told him. He jerked around. The breeze ruffled his dark hair and he squinted up at her.

"I'm not going to sit next to you," she continued "because you switch moods so fast I don't want to be close. You might shake my head clean off before I have a chance to get away, then shout something at me about Sara Lee Banana Cake."

"I guess I deserve that," he said, then pursed his lips. "What can I say?"

"You can promise to mind your p's and q's, and behave yourself."

"All right. I promise. Now sit here and tell me all about yourself. Tell it all. Spare no detail."

"You're doing it again."

"What? What am I doing?"

"You're getting snippy."

"You're right, Theresa. I'm sorry. I do want to hear all about you, though."

"There's not much to tell."

He patted the stair again and she said, "Move over."

He scooted and she sat.

"When I was in high school," she began, "I used to spend the summers helping out at the old Indian Mission here on the island—right next to the ferry slip on the south end. They're not there anymore. They've moved over to the mainland—I don't know what's there now. You've seen the place, haven't you? Maybe not, not if you have your own boat."

"Oh, I've seen it. Go on."

"Well, I used to peel potatoes and set tables. Later on I was a camp counselor. Are you sure you want to hear all this?"

He nodded.

"They used to bring Indian kids in from all over the province. We had clam bakes and wiener roasts. Sort of a combination of cultures, eh? I even lifeguarded one summer. I enjoyed that. Plus I got a good tan."

"That's it?"

"That's it," she said and slapped her hands on her thighs.

"You call *that* being a missionary?" He started to laugh and buried his head between his knees.

"Oh, my goodness," he moaned, rocking, his nose tucked down by his shoes. Theresa stared at him. The man was totally unpredictable.

"You promised," she reminded him. "You promised—"

"I'm not laughing at you. I'm laughing at *me!* Want to hear something funny? I wasn't going to tell you, but I might as well. I was more of a missionary than you! But why am I telling you this?"

"What are you talking about?"

"Young Life. Ever hear of it?"

Of course she had. The high school version of Campus Crusade. Four spiritual laws and all that.

"I used to be a leader," he said, rubbing his head hard, staring at the ground below the steps. "Can you believe it? I used to have a bunch of kids at Queen Anne High in Seattle. Did the whole routine. Singing in the winter, witnessing in the spring, sailing in the summer . . ."

"So who's calling who a Jesus freak? You're more of one than I am!"

"Not any more, lady. It's all over. Come on." He stood and offered her his hand. "Got any coffee around here?"

"Instant."

"That'll work. Tell me where and I'll fix it."

"That's okay. I can get it."

"I *know* you can get it. But go on. Here, pull up a stump and sit down." He waved grandly to the fat stump at the bottom of the steps, and he brushed the dirt from it gallantly. "You sit here, and I'll bring it out to you."

"Shawn—"

"I insist."

There was a lot more to this man than met the eye. He said he hated fanatics, but had a religious background that apparently outdid hers. And he wiped dirty tables and made coffee for women.

Inside, the cupboard doors clanked and rattled. There was the sound of running water.

"The last man who brought me coffee had to have been my father!" she called, sitting carefully on the stump. It was pleasantly warm.

"And when was that?"

Like a heavy cloud rolling over the horizon on a blue day, it was all ruined. She shouldn't have said anything. "I guess it would have to be eight years ago," she said. "That's when they died."

He came to the door and leaned against the frame. "Your folks are dead?"

"Mm-m."

"I'm sorry."

"It was a long time ago."

"What happened?"

"Well, it was a long time ago."

"You mean you don't want to talk about it." He stood, waiting.

"They were killed in an automobile accident," she said at last. "A drunk slammed into them."

"You sound bitter."

"I'm not."

"Sure you are. I can hear it in your voice."

"You know something?" she flared again, feeling angry, yet surprised that he knew which buttons to push. "I think *you're* the one who's bitter. And you hide it all in some gobbledygook about the company God keeps. At least I know why *I'm* mad at God."

"See? You *are* mad at God!"

"Mad and bitter are two different things, Shawn Malone—in case you didn't know."

"I hear the teakettle. Be back in a minute."

He brought out the coffee on a tray, with stale biscuits. He handed her the Royal Albert Country Rose teacup she'd used yesterday.

62

"Thanks," she said and curled one hand around the cup. What a different morning this was!

He sat three feet from her on the bottom step. "You're welcome," he replied.

Then they said nothing for several minutes. Two squirrels chased up a tree, chattering and screeching. A snake slithered out of the grass a few feet away. A lizard crept out to a flat rock and sat still.

"What was Lover Boy like?"

Theresa jumped. A bit of the coffee sloshed into the saucer.

"Why do you keep calling him that?"

"What was he like?" he asked again.

"You've seen his picture."

He chuckled. "I guess I have." The chuckle grew.

"*Now* what's so funny?" As if she didn't know.

"That's what I call throwing someone in your face!" He laughed out loud and reached up to the railing. Before she had time to think, he'd pulled the broken frame down and had it in his lap.

"He's not a bad-looking guy," he said, then turned the picture over. "Did you know there's a message written on the back of this? Just like in the good spy novels!"

A sick little knot tightened in her stomach. "Give it to me."

"Let's see. It says, *Dear Theresa—*"

"Give it to me. Please."

He handed it to her and she put it aside, surprised at how easily he gave it up.

"Do you know what it says?" he asked.

"No."

"Aren't you going to read it?"

"No."

"Why not?"

"Why should I?"

"Maybe it's the key to buried treasure or something."

She glared at him.

"Go on. Read it."

"No."

"Okay, have it your way. Say, are you Canadian?"

"Yes. Why?"

"Just wondered. Trying to make conversation. It's getting a little heated around here again—or hadn't you noticed?"

She set her cup on the stump and, carrying the picture, slipped past him up the stairs. He caught her ankle and she tugged. "Let me go."

"Where are you going?"

"I'm going to put this picture inside."

"What if I don't let you go?"

The barbecue sat right beside the back door. She might just be able to reach it. Shawn held her fast and she had to stretch and strain, but by lying flat against the steps and reaching with her left hand, she could just barely poke it underneath—out of sight. Riddance to rubbish.

"Now will you let me go?" she asked.

"Are you going to sit on your stump?"

"I am."

"All right. I'll let you go."

She rubbed the two spots where her shins had rubbed against the stair edges, then hobbled down the steps and picked up what was left of her coffee.

"Where did you grow up?" he asked. "Vancouver?"

"A little town just outside called Port Coquitlam. Are you from Seattle?"

64

"Born and bred."

"I moved there about four years ago."

"No kidding? What are you doing up here?"

"Holiday."

It wasn't a real holiday she knew. She was supposed to be getting some of her writing done. And since she'd needed to get away after the breakup with Ron, her professor at the University of Washington had given her an independent study. She was supposed to come up with a book outline and finish two short stories. *And* forget Ron.

"Why did he dump you?"

"Did it ever occur to you I might not want to talk about him?"

"How come he dumped you?"

"How do you know he dumped me? Maybe I dumped him."

"I don't think you'd have been calling out his name when you were drowning, or throwing his picture around, if you had dumped him. It's elementary, my dear Watson."

"So who are you, a detective or something?"

"I must be something because I'm not a detective."

"You're a creep," she laughed, ducking a small twig that he tossed.

"And you love it. No, I'm not a detective, but I read a lot of detective stories. But tell me, Theresa, what caused the breakup?"

He scooted around and leaned against the porch rail. Since his legs were too long, he had to draw them up at the knees. "Ah. . . . This is the life." He squinted one eye open. "Am I nosy?"

"You're nosy."

"But you want to tell me. I can tell."

He was really too audacious to suit her, but then Ron's line popped into mind and she couldn't resist. "It was God's will we break up."

She was pleased to see both Shawn's eyes pop open and his back yank free of the post.

"Are you serious?"

"That's what he said," she told him.

"What was the real reason?"

She knew he wouldn't fall for it. "Another woman. I found out the truth. Younger, too. Educated. Without freckles."

"I like your freckles."

"You do?"

"I *love* your freckles."

He could make her laugh, and she took the last sip of cold coffee. "She was tall."

"I like my women petite."

"Slender—"

"Not near as slender as you."

"Gorgeous."

"You're gorgeous."

"Stunning."

"You're stunning."

"Witty, wise, and wonderful."

"You're witty, wise, and wonderful."

How come he could make her laugh? She leaned over to set her empty cup on the bottom step. He set his down right next to it and touched the handles together. Their eyes locked. When he bumped the handles and made a click, she blinked.

"So instead of just telling you he didn't love you anymore," he said, "the creep just said it was God's will."

"That's about it."

"And you're wasting your time crying over this jerk?"

Memories of Shawn's kiss splashed in her head and Theresa swallowed. "Not anymore."

"Well, I've got to be going," he said.

"So suddenly?"

He rose and stretched and carried the two cups inside. She scrambled to her feet after him. "Now?"

"Yeah, I think so."

"Please don't."

"I think I'd better. You keep the groceries, though. I bought them for you."

"Shawn?" He thumped down the steps.

"Shawn? Your sweatshirt, Shawn!" she called, grabbing it off the rail.

He stopped, then turned slowly to face her. She approached him with the thud of her heart in her throat.

"Thanks," he said, and started to go again.

"Will I see you again?" she asked faintly.

"I don't know."

"What do you mean, you don't know?"

"I guess I just don't know."

"Please, Shawn—"

He kissed her quickly, but it took her breath away.

"I don't like fanatics," he said, holding her at arm's length. "I really don't."

"I'm not a fanatic," she whispered. "I've told you that."

He stood in knee-length grasses. The branch of a birch tree hung low and blocked his face.

"Theresa," he said with an air of finality, "anybody who says a prayer over cold eggs has got to be a fanatic."

The last she saw of him was a patch of blue jacket disappearing through the trees. A fanatic. Hardly the way she'd describe herself.

She returned to the warm stump to think.

CHAPTER 5

ONLY TWO DAYS AT Thetis and what did she have to show for it? Broken eggshells all over her counter, a bashed-in head, and two men to cry about.

Well, she wasn't going to cry about Shawn. And the picture of Ron could stay where it was. Buried treasure. . . . Shawn had a sorry sense of humor. No doubt the message on the back was some romantic fancy of Ron's from the old days, and she certainly didn't want to see it now.

Well, what was she going to do? This getaway was not an excuse to do nothing. There was the cabin to clean and her writing to get at. Professor Sorenson, the one who'd designed an independent study for her in Short Story, wanted a new twist to the one she'd contracted to complete. It was too predictable. Sorenson was right.

But right now there was the mess in the kitchen. "Where do I start?" she asked out loud, throwing up her arms, spinning in a complete circle. There was everything to do. Curtains to be taken down. Blankets to be shaken. Vacuuming to be done. Cupboards to be cleaned.

She poked through the grocery bags Shawn had brought over. *He's an interesting guy, Mr. Shawn Malone,* she thought, pulling out bananas and a bag of fresh peaches. Following her home like that, sneaking in, getting breakfast ready. He really was a nice guy— but he could surely switch moods fast.

She remembered the kisses. *Don't think about it. Get at the cleaning and then pull out the old typewriter.*

Her typewriter was a blue one—a portable Smith Corona—a high school graduation present from her uncle. He'd gotten it for her because he said she was going to be a great writer. Well, she was a writer; great was still in the making.

Maybe if she worked hard and got the bulk of the cleaning done, she could work outside on the front patio before supper. And nibble on the potato chips Shawn had brought. Potato chips and boiled eggs. Not a great supper, but it would do.

She tackled the work straightway, scrubbing mouse droppings and cobwebs from the empty cupboards, tearing out old shelf lining, laying down fresh newspaper. Auntie Sue would appreciate her work, too, she knew. She tried to concentrate on her plot, but once in a while thoughts of Shawn popped up, which she resolutely pushed aside. At times Ron popped up—in painful ways. When she knocked over the brown sugar in the blue Tupperware jug, she remembered the night they'd made scotchies, and how he'd teased her and kissed the back of her neck while she wiped up the mess. Now she bit her lip and refused to think about it. Time, she told herself, would heal all wounds. That's what her mother used to say, and although she doubted it, there was nothing else to hang on to.

At teatime she took a break and sat out on the front porch. Her neighbor was rowing out to his boat and she waved. He waved back. Her father had helped him put the buoy in, on a day very much like this. Clean, with warm sun. Just a little breeze.

They could still be here if it were not for that drunken driver. They could be sitting at the picnic table right now, playing Scrabble—Mum knitting, Dad chewing on a toothpick. But no, it was just she. And it was so quiet.

Tea over, she scrubbed a stubborn spot of what looked like spilled honey on the shelf between the stove and sink, still thinking about her folks. She scrubbed harder and harder. She watched the cleanser turn blue in the sink. She swept and wiped and straightened. She wiped her eyes and took deep breaths. She moved on to the bedroom.

She slipped the faded yellow priscillas from the rod, then pulled the layers of blankets off the bed and stripped away the sheets. An old red sock fell out from somewhere and she threw it angrily in the pile of the yellow curtains to be washed.

They could be working on this together. Mum could be mopping, Dad cleaning out the closets. In fact, if they were still alive, she wouldn't have had to go live with her aunt and uncle and she wouldn't have fallen in love with Ron and—

Stop it. Just stop it, she told herself. *You're thinking irrationally, and feeling sorry for yourself.*

Something had happened out on the front porch

during tea. Or maybe it was just being here, surrounded by so much that was her folks and Ron, that stirred old feelings and pain—like a feather duster busy in a dusty attic. Only instead of getting a cleaned-up attic, she was stirring up a lot of things she didn't like.

Lugging the blankets out to the front porch, she leaned over the rail and shook out each one, sneezing and squinting her eyes to the great poofs of dust and sand that flew free.

Thoughts shook loose in her head, too. And the more she thought about things, the more they flew about. She snapped the blankets the way her mother used to, and reveled in the sound of the heavy covers snapping, snapping, snapping. A seagull cawed overhead.

She was putting the blankets and new sheets on the bed when she noticed the nail on the bedroom wall. There it was. Big and rusty and jabbing a full inch out of the wall. The brewing anger exploded. Why had they hung his picture up, anyway? It was a rather cruel thing to do.

Ron did not write anything on the back of that picture. They did. The realization slammed into her head like a rock bouncing off a cliff, and she sat on the bed to consider. They had known she would take the picture down, and in the process discover the note. But why the picture? Why not just a note on the kitchen counter? In order to be theatrical? Why so unkind? Her aunt and uncle were not mean.

I am not going to read that message.

The stump in the backyard was hot when Theresa sat down, and Ron's eyes, distorted by the shattered glass, stared up at her. For a long time she stared back, fighting the impulse to turn the frame in her hand. *Buried treasure*.

"Dear Theresa," she read, in spite of herself. "We left the picture because we're concerned that you'll do as you've done in the past, and that is to ignore your feelings instead of working through them." Biting her lip, she continued to read. "Maybe this way, seeing Ron's picture, you'll have to come to grips with how you *really* feel. We're afraid that you'll carry this pain forever, as you're doing with your folks. We hoped, maybe by seeing his picture, you would at least cry."

Cry. That's all she ever did. Now a lump grew hard in her throat as fresh tears threatened. In time Ron's face grew fuzzy and it was her father's eyes she saw. Then her mother's. Then she heard the crunch, the squeal of tires. She squeezed the picture hard in her fingers while the truth of what her aunt and uncle had said jumped up and down in her head like springs gone haywire. She did carry her pain around. But what else was she supposed to do with it?

Outside the day was still clean and the sun still warm. There was more on the back of the picture and she read slowly:

"We're sorry it's our son who has hurt you. We hope and pray you can find your way through this—perhaps the rest and time away will help. We hope so. And remember, there is probably somebody else out there for you. Somebody more like you. Love, Auntie Sue and Uncle John."

Seagulls screeched, and far off she heard the buzz of an outboard. Close at hand she could feel the thud of her own heartbeat in the base of her throat. Someone else? Not likely. She and Ron were made for each other.

But what about Shawn? The tall, handsome stranger who kissed and teased so tenderly. But who could speak so unkindly, too, she reminded herself. Shawn was just a tall, romantic image, with all the idiosyncrasies romantic images brought with them. She and Shawn would never be as close as she and Ron had been. Besides, he may have written her off already. He hated fanatics. And while she didn't understand much about God these days, she had to admit that deep down, she probably was a fanatic. She and Shawn were poles apart spiritually.

It gave her a warm, comfortable feeling to think about Sunday morning hymns and cups of coffee and friends to visit, and God talked of and talked to. It gave her a warm, comfortable feeling to say grace over cold eggs, even if it did bother Shawn. Deep down she knew that God held the answers. It was a matter of muddling through somehow until she could find what those answers were.

It was all so mixed-up. She didn't know what she thought or felt anymore. Her eye caught Uncle John's postscript down in the very corner of the picture: "God collects our tears in a bottle. Psalm 56:8."

God collected tears? In a bottle? The way her aunt collected agates? For another second she looked at the strong handwriting, so much like her father's, then dashed inside to find a Bible. There had to be one somewhere.

She found it on the third shelf of the bookrack, between *A Cup Of Gold* and *Franny and Zooey*. One of those old-fashioned kind with the zipper—the kind they gave out at Sunday school for memory work. "Thou hast kept count of my tossings; put thou my tears in thy bottle!"

The thought struck her forceably: that God actually collected *tears*, and He put them in bottles! Her writers' mind saw them lined up on a kitchen windowsill with names taped to each one. Probably taped with adhesive tape, the way her mother used to identify canned food. Then it dawned on her that God must have a lot of bottles!

The milk bottle on her aunt's kitchen windowsill was full of agates. Sunlight reflected off the rocks. A strange quiet came to Theresa as she stood at the sink, and for a long time she turned the bottle, watching the light come and go among the rocks, letting the quiet work its way deep. Although no answers came, she felt an odd sense of peace that perhaps maybe God *was* there, that maybe she was not so mistreated after all. "And the peace of God which passeth all understanding shall keep your hearts and minds. . . ." She'd memorized that verse as a child.

"Are you *really* saving my tears, God?" she whispered. "Do you know how painful it still is to think about them? Do you know how jilted I feel because Ron—"

I must be going crazy. I've never talked out loud to God before.

It was getting on toward six o'clock. The shadows had grown long, and the tide had come in. It was nearly the end of the day and she'd gotten no writing done.

"There's always the evening," she said to no one in particular. "No, forget the story. Boil the eggs and get out the potato chips for supper. Treat yourself. Write in your journal."

Boy, I really must be going crazy, talking out loud like this.

She put the eggs on to boil and headed for the shower, anxious now to get at her journal. Sometimes writing out her feelings helped solidify them, made them take a shape she could recognize.

The hot water felt good on her back. She shampooed her hair, careful not to bump the sore on her head, rinsed, and added conditioner. Reluctantly she turned the taps to off and stood shivering in the stall. She'd forgotten to get a towel.

There were actually cobwebs on the shoulder of Uncle John's old bathrobe. Shivering and grimacing, she swiped at the webs, pulled the robe down, then wriggled into it. Her wild scream frightened her just as badly as it frightened the family of mice. They fell from the bathrobe pocket, out a side hole, and two little babies the size of large peanuts sprawled on the floor just beyond her toes. The mother scurried out of sight, the end of her tail whipping around the back leg of the old dresser that sat beneath the window.

Theresa shivered, repulsed, then in a panic checked the pocket for more. No more. Just a pile of shredded stuff that was apparently the nest. The squeak, squeak on the floor checked her panic, and she knelt curiously to see the tiny creatures whose eyes were not yet even open.

"Oh, you're so *cute!*" she exclaimed, rubbing the edge of her finger along the side of their bodies. Tiny paw fingers spread. They tumbled and skittered in useless circles, their eyes still shut tight. "But, oh, you need your mother!"

"Here, Mouse," she called, stooping to investigate under the dresser. A hole led to the outside, and through it she saw a bit of grass and rocky ground.

"There goes that idea," she said, still talking to the

two squeaking, frantic babies. "What's the matter? You hungry?"

Her own stomach growled furiously. It had been a long time ago that she and Shawn had eaten those cold eggs, and she'd been cleaning all afternoon with only a cup of tea and a couple of biscuits to fortify her.

In the medicine cabinet she found a good-sized safety pin and secured the pocket of Uncle John's bathrobe. Then, nervous at first but feeling rather noble and heroic, she picked up the mice gently and settled them back into her pocket.

"There now," she crooned. "I'll get you some milk. Hush now. You wait."

But Shawn hadn't brought any milk. And the eggs were jumping wildly in the pan. She turned off the stove. She would have to go down to the marina after all. She could get an eyedropper while she was there.

She put on her favorite casual outfit. The gray flannel sweatshirt with lavender sleeves and lavender letters spelled out *Washington* across the chest. Ron had given her the shirt when she'd started taking writing courses at the university, and it matched her lavender slacks perfectly. Well, Ron had turned out to be a bust, but the classes hadn't, and her professor apparently thought she had potential.

She grabbed a baggy white sweater from behind the water heater and checked the mice twice. They'd found each other and squealed fright and comfort to each other.

"Be good now," she murmured. "I'll be back as soon as I can."

She walked with a spring to her step. Forgotten were the day's frustrations, Ron's picture, and Shawn. The night air was sweet with summer fragrance. Frogs croaked in the ditches. Crickets chirped.

The marina was full of activity, and Mr. McCullough seemed glad to see her. He asked her how she was and what was it that she needed.

"The bump on your head, it's looking better," he observed, tapping his own forehead. "What you need that eyedropper for?"

"To feed some baby mice. They fell out of my uncle's bathrobe just now and the mother ran off."

Mr. McCullough sighed. "You think they like allsorts?" he asked.

So they were going to continue the game, and she was going to gain too much weight playing along. She smiled.

"I think they probably just might," she said, nodding her head at him. He dropped the licorice into her bag. "They'll love 'em. And thanks." She reached for the grocery bag.

"Ah, it's nothing, eh? By the way," he called to her as she headed for the door. "If you're lookin' for that American, don't bother. He's gone."

She leaned against the doorjamb, half in the store, half out, clutching her shopping bag. "You mean Shawn?"

"The very same."

"Gone?" she repeated.

Three children argued over popsicles in a corner and their mother tattered at them. They paid no heed and kept up the racket. Not until now had Theresa realized she'd been hoping to see him. It was why she'd put on her favorite outfit—as if she were in junior high again and the boy she liked hadn't noticed her hair out of pigtails yet.

"Gone? When did he go?" she asked weakly.

"Oh, this side o' noon, I'm thinkin'. No, maybe

more like three. Nope. It was this side o' noon, eh? I remember now."

"Did he say where he was going?"

"Nope. Just that he was off."

"Did he leave a message or anything?"

"Seems you've grown mighty attached all of a sudden here, lassie."

She blushed under his frank stare. "Mr. McCullough?"

"Yes, lassie?"

"Did he say if he was coming back?"

"That he didn't." Absently Mr. McCullough took the coins from the children and they darted out past Theresa. "It's all you can expect from an American, lass," he added, ringing up the register.

She just wanted to be outside, away from everyone and everything. She backed out the door, bag in her arms.

"Well, if it's more all-sorts you want, you know where to come and get them, don't you, lass?"

"Yes. And thanks." She tried to smile.

The door shut behind her and she could hear the wild clatter of Mr. McCullough's bells. There was no tall mast beside Dock E. No tall mast anywhere out there.

CHAPTER 6

THE WALK HOME WAS LONG. Theresa's bag of groceries grew heavier with each step. So Shawn had gone off and left her. Just sailed in, then sailed out of her life. She tried to force herself to walk faster. How long did mice survive without food when they were that young? Shawn? He'd just up and left, just like that. The mice, she had to hurry. How could he do it? After barging in on her life the way he had, then just dropping out of sight. Well, one thing was plain. Whatever he did, he did with a bang. The mice. She had to get back and feed the mice.

She was trying to ignore it again, wasn't she? Ignoring the pain and her feelings. It was just like her aunt and uncle had written. It must be a pattern of hers. Here she was, concentrating on some silly little mice that fell out of a dusty bathrobe, just so she didn't have to fact up to the fact that she was angry and hurt and feeling horribly, horribly lonely—over a man she hardly knew.

And not only lonely, she had to admit, but more like abandoned. That's *really* how she felt. Abandoned—just like the baby mice in her uncle's pocket. The same feeling she got when she thought of her folks. And Ron. That she'd been suddenly left behind. And now, here she was feeling that way with Shawn. Like a child stuck at home while everybody else got to go to the fair.

In a rush she realized it was exactly how she had felt with God, too. He'd abandoned her because He'd let all those things happen. That's why she'd liked that verse so much today about God collecting her tears. It meant He hadn't abandoned her after all.

Too much to think about. Shadows lengthened and she hurried on, wondering. The night chill penetrated her *Washington* sweatshirt and thin sweater. Abandonment. Two baby mice in a pocket. Now *that* was abandonment. Mum just running off, escaping out a back hole.

Turning off the main road into the cabin's driveway—just a swath of overgrown grass between thick trees—Theresa stumbled over hidden roots and small stones. Had it been only this morning that she and Shawn had stood out here and he'd said he didn't know if he'd see her again? Why was she so surprised, then, that he was gone?

The mound of dirty laundry greeted her when she slid through the back door—and faint squeaks from the bathroom. Wasting no time, she turned on the stove and poured a small bit of Mr. McCullough's milk into a saucepan. At first she'd thought one had died, but by wrapping it in cotton batting and forcing the warm milk into its mouth, she was able to squeeze a few drops in. The second feeding was easier. And by the third feeding, both of them were opening their mouths on their own, sucking greedily, tiny paws clutching the dropper.

Every two hours all night long Theresa got up to warm more milk and wondered why she was doing it. They were only mice, after all. *Mice!* She hated mice. She was scared of mice.

But they were so cute. And helpless. And nearly dead.

When morning came, sunlight spilling quietly into the windows, Theresa stirred softly, thought of the mice, looked at the alarm, then snuggled back down under the covers. She had another half-hour. The next time she woke the clock was shrieking.

It was a pretty morning. The familiar sea chill in the air put goosebumps on your legs, but felt wonderful. Mechanically Theresa went through the motions of feeding the mice and getting her own breakfast on the table—the boiled eggs she was supposed to have had for dinner the night before. Her forehead was sticky, but the mirror and a cautious dabbing, told her that the swelling was down and that the gash was scabbing over. The smaller scratches already seemed to be on the mend, and a couple of aspirins chased away the dull headache. There was nothing to do but unfold a lawn chair and get at her journal—which she'd totally forgotten about the night before.

She set the chair outside on the patio where she could see the sea. It was an old chair, with wooden bars and canvas seating—the only one left from early days at Grandpa's house on Fraser Street. It was her favorite. She fixed a pot of tea, brought out Mr. McCullough's all-sorts, and in the rising warmth of the new day began scribbling random thoughts into her notebook, snaring the elusive emotions and feelings that darted in and out like slippery eels. She wrote fast and furiously, becoming captured by her own discoveries.

"What does it mean to be abandoned?" she wrote. "Babies are abandoned on orphanage steps. In New York they're left in garbage cans. Can grownups be abandoned, too, in the sense that if no one comes along and finds them on top of the soggy celery and empty tin cans, they will die? As if Shawn had left me to drown?"

She recalled the story of Moses in the bullrushes, then later on, grown up, leading the people of Israel through the desert for forty years. "Does God abandon his people?" she wrote. "Moses must have felt abandoned. Jesus must have, too. 'Father, why hast thou forsaken me?' "

But God had not abandoned His Son. It had only *felt* like it. Theresa chewed on the end of her pen, watching the tide turn. The sun climbed, the tide receded, and she lost track of time. She went inside for the Bible and became engrossed in the portions someone had underlined.

"For I know the plans I have for you," says the Lord, "plans for welfare and not for evil, to give you a future and a hope."

That was Jeremiah 29:11. God had a future for her? That didn't sound like abandonment. Funny, up until now she hadn't thought much about a future—for herself, that is—other than just being married to Ron. It had always been Ron's future. Working for Ron. Praying for Ron. Waiting for Ron. Did God really have a future for Theresa?

Sunlight glinted off a piece of broken glass in the yard. A chipmunk darted up the trunk of a Douglas fir. Then she caught sight of something out of the corner of her eye, and turned just in time to see a mouse disappearing through a knothole under the porch. With a quick leap, she was out of her chair and pressing her eye to the hole. But she could see nothing in the dark below.

In the afternoon Theresa stuffed all the laundry into a pillowcase—dirty rags and dusty curtains, doilies and dish towels. Grabbing one of Shawn's bananas, she set off down the back road toward the marina and Mr. McCullough's laundromat. Jeremiah 29:11 and Psalm 56:8 echoed in her head.

There was no sign of *The Sailing Bear* at the marina and she swallowed a taste of disappointment. Again she hadn't realized she'd been hoping so badly.

The reds and blues and yellows and whites flopped and turned behind the glass of the large laundromat dryers. Round and round, falling, and back around, over and over. *Just the way we live our days*, she thought, staring at the clothes.

A sudden urge to be out doing something, anything, drove her from her chair and last year's magazines.

Mr. McCullough's bells jangled pleasantly when she entered the store. "How're you doing out there?" he greeted her. "You're looking your usual self."

"I'm fine, thanks. Doing the laundry today."

"How are those mice?"

She laughed. "I know it's silly, but I could hardly let them die."

"You finish up those all-sorts already?" She laughed again. "You'll be needing to put a bit o' weight on your bones, anyway. How about a few more, eh?"

"Well, I really came in to see if I could borrow a fishing rod, or even just a line, if you have one."

"You ever hear anything from that Ron o' yours?"

"No, but he's not my Ron, Mr. McCullough. Do you have a fishing pole?"

"And what you be needing a fishing pole for?"

"I thought I might take a walk down to the ferry slip while I'm waiting for the laundry. See if I can't catch some supper."

"Ferry slip, eh?" he grunted, digging a pole out of a back closet. "You seen what they done to the old mission when you come in?"

"I didn't look real hard, to tell you the truth. The fresh coat of paint, that was obvious. Do you know who owns the place now?"

"Capernwray Harbor. Another Christian outfit. Bible school or something. Surprised you don't know about it. Doing a real nice job with the place, too. Say, you might want to go down and introduce yourself—have a real good look-see." He handed her the pole. "And here's some salmon eggs for bait, or were you planning on talking them in? Let me know what the insides look like, eh?"

"Of the *fish?*"

His laughter was one of those bellyfulls. "Heavens, no! The insides of the new outfit over there!"

"Sure. If I do, I will." Biting the bag of licorice, she tore the package open and chose one of the layered kinds. She held the bag out to Mr. McCullough, but he declined with a broad shake of his head.

"Well, I'll be seeing you then," she said. "And thank you."

85

"You're welcome, eh?"

She smiled to herself, pole in one hand. *You've been in Seattle too long,* she told herself. *It's nice to be home.*

The ferry slip was located on the very south end of the island, right next to the old North American Indian Mission, a refurbished estate from way back, and the new public wharf. The two docks and the mission house met the few people who found their way to the island. To Theresa, the two docks and the mission house were what Thetis Island *was.* Her uncle's cabin and the marina were really only appendages, like the lean-to bathroom on the cabin. Now that she was on her way she was anxious to get there. She had spent so many good times at the Mission.

Protected from the morning sun, the beach still had dew on the ground. She felt the dampness seep through her running shoes. The arbutus trees hung over the cliffs, their dark red bark peeling and twisting off in ribbons. The crushed barnacles along the shore glistened as the sun made its way overhead, and Theresa stopped occasionally to check out a tide pool, to see if there were any starfish.

But there were none, so with fishing pole over her shoulder, she kept walking and breathed in the rich scent of Thetis—the salt air, the seaweed, and the mussel shells. Without realizing it, she slipped back into an old game, hopping from log to log, trying to see how far she could get without stepping off a piece of driftwood. It had been years since she'd done it. Then she came around the corner and there it was.

The public wharf was first, stretched beyond the mud flats so that the end was well over the water, even at low tide. It was a sturdy structure, newer than the ferry slip, which was old and soggy and rotting away despite the creosote and repairs. The docks sat about fifty yards apart looking like old man and son. The *Thetis Island* sign framed the off-ramp of the ferry slip like a decorated goalpost on a football field, and through the "goal post" Theresa could see the stately mansion of the old North American Indian Mission.

She'd put in a lot of summers. All through high school she'd worked there. One summer Ron had worked for the mission, too, only he had been a volunteer student through their Summer Missionary Institute. They sent teams of college students out to various Indian villages with the sole purpose of setting up new churches and establishing Bible studies. Ron had gone to Chase, way up in the interior, and she had missed him terribly, but had kept busy peeling potatoes and setting tables and playing with the Indian children who had come for summer camp.

Standing on the wharf now, looking at the old mansion, she thought back to those days. They had been good days, and seeing the place again, she remembered them easily. But those days were gone. She couldn't stand here dreaming about them. Everything was different now. It wasn't the Indian Mission anymore. It was something else.

What had Mr. McCullough said was the name of the new outfit? The fresh coat of white paint on the main building—a stately two-story structure with dormers along the front—was striking. In its beginning the mansion had had a span in the middle where the horses had been brought in with the carriage. Now the room was filled in. When the Indian Mission had owned it, the room had been a lobby, the south wing being the kitchen and dining hall and small offices, the north wing being the chapel and meeting hall. She wondered what it was like now.

The call of two boys arrested her attention. They were dangling over the edge of the wharf, heads hanging.

"It's starting to grow!" shouted the smaller of the two, who wore red shorts and running shoes the color of mud.

"I told you!" the other exclaimed. "Look it!" He wiggled in excitement, inching himself further over the edge.

Theresa, curiosity piqued, went over to them, leaning so she could see what it was that was so fascinating.

"You gotta get down!" the smaller boy hollered. "You gotta lie down and look up underneath if you wanna see it."

The splintery planks were warm and smelled rich with salt and oil and dust. "What are you looking at?"

"The starfish my dad cut up."

She recoiled, pulling away automatically. "What?"

"Ah, it's nothin'," the little boy said, three teeth missing out of his smile. "He cut off one of the legs. It's our summer experiment. Our dad is a scientist. He said that starfishes can grow their legs back on but people can't."

"Oh."

"Come on, take a look. It's growin' real neat!" Theresa bent over obediently and looked under the pier to where the two boys pointed. The supporting pilings, covered with barnacles and creosote and seaweed, seemed to be a haven for purple starfish.

Fifteen or twenty clung to the posts, stuck firmly by the miniature suction cups beneath them.

"Where?" she asked, searching the gloomy dark.

"There! Over there!"

"Where?"

"Over there, by the two that look tangled up."

She saw it. Four appendages, with a stub.

"You see it?"

"Yes, I see it."

"Our dad says it'll be all grown on in a few weeks and it'll be as good as new."

Just like broken hearts? she wondered. *Do they mend?* She sat up, momentarily dizzy from the thought—and the rush of blood to her head.

"What's the matter? You got a pain?"

"No. Just a little dizzy, is all. Say, would you guys like to help me fish? It's been a long time and I've sort of forgotten how."

"Gee!" glowed the smaller of the boys. "Ya hear that, Charles? She said we—"

"You gonna share your all-sorts?" interrupted the older.

"Sure. Fair's fair, eh?"

"Fair's fair. Sure, we'll help you." They poked the salmon eggs onto her rusty hook and took turns casting out.

The ferry came and went, dropping off and picking up six cars and a few passengers. It was a small ferry, one that dipped and took the waves with splashes and vigor. The sun climbed higher into the sky, sometimes dodging behind large, cumulus clouds, putting a shadow over them and the fish they were catching.

"Where do you fellows live?" Theresa asked, chewing on yet another of Mr. McCullough's licorices, her laundry completely forgotten. She had chosen a pink speckled piece, rolling it around on her teeth as the beads melted, leaving just the jellied licorice underneath.

"Over there," said Charles, pointing in the direction of the ferry slip.

"The Indian Mission?"

"No. Capernwray Harbor."

Capernwray Harbor, that was it. "You fellows live there? No kidding."

"Our dad is in charge."

"In charge, eh? Say, you fellows wouldn't like to show me around, would you? I used to work there, when it was the Indian Mission. I'd like to see the old place again. Do you still have that old trampoline in the barn?"

"You used to work there?" whistled Charles.

"Yeah, about six years ago. I worked in the kitchen. Peeling potatoes," she added and laughed.

"We have to do that sometimes," said Frederick, the smaller boy. He pulled in the line and picked up the fish, catching them through the gills with his fingers.

Charles picked up the other two. "Come on, we'll show you around, won't we, Frederick?"

"Sure."

"Do you still have that trampoline?" she asked again.

"What trampoline?"

"The one up in the barn."

"Nothin' up there but a pile 'a horse poop."

"Frederick!" scolded the older boy. Frederick shrugged.

"Guess the Mission took it," Theresa said.

They walked abreast along the bit of road that passed the ferry slip and ended at the old mission grounds, then went single-file along the trail that had been beaten down by two little boys taking shortcuts.

The rockery was what she noticed first. The whole front lawn had been raised and a beautiful rockery had been put in. Zinnias, marigolds, flowers she didn't know the names of, gave bright color. In the distance was a huge garden—a miniature farm, really—with more marigolds planted throughout, splashing more color around.

"What do you want to see first, the kitchen?" asked Charles.

"Well, maybe you'd better ask your dad first," she suggested, thinking twice now about the idea of a personal tour. She almost felt like a trespasser, although the place seemed to welcome her as if she'd come home.

"Ah, it's okay," said Charles. "There isn't anybody here now anyway. It's between quarters and it's just the main crew. Dad won't mind a bit."

By this time they had approached the old mansion. Theresa touched the building, the cool plaster and fresh paint. The windows sparkled. And as they rounded the corner to the back, a wave of nostalgia hit and she had to blink back the tears.

The old carriage span—the converted lobby—looked just the same; only instead of a pink, frayed chesterfield and blond end-tables along one wall, there was an attractive leather chesterfield and several bookcases. The large picture of Jesus was gone. In its place hung a pastoral scene of sheep and a shepherd's tent. Serenity enveloped the room, and she noted that it was clean and tidy, unlike the mission days when help was short and time never long enough.

Deep voices interrupted by throaty laughs came from the south wing, where the offices and kitchen had been.

"The kitchen this way?" she asked, moving in that direction. She was anxious to see if the huge sinks were still there, and if the maze of back closets were still tangled and messy and fun to get lost in. Bright green gingham curtains lined the windows looking out over the water.

"Yeah. Frederick, you take her in while I do something with these fish. Mum'll kill me if I slop up the floor. Want me to clean yours, Theresa?"

"Sure."

She followed Frederick and his red shorts and mud shoes down the short hallway that led to a center room. Smaller rooms to the right, the kitchen to the left, more of the gingham curtains. "Freddie? Maybe you'd better take me in and introduce me to your father."

"It's Frederick. And I think he's with somebody." The little boy was thoughtful, listening to the muffled conversation from behind a partially closed door.

"Frederick? Charles? Is that you out there?" Then, "Come on, Ron, I want to introduce you to my kids."

Ron? She could hear the footsteps on the old floor and with each sound a numbing cold took hold. *Some other Ron.*

There was no place to hide. She stepped backward, dizzy from no breath, her heart thudding behind her ears. She knew she had to sit or she would faint, and there was no chair. Sunlight filtered through sheer curtains, and there he was.

And he looked just the same.

CHAPTER 7

COLD DROPPED INTO the pit of Theresa's stomach, then spread. Her feet froze first and she was caught, staring into blue, blue eyes and the smile she knew so well.

"Hello, Theresa."

She shivered. "Hello, Ron."

The cold inside thawed to an instant heat that made her feel faint, and she turned from his eyes.

"How do you do," she mumbled, trying to focus on the other man in front of her. He was a large man, with powerful shoulders and a barrel chest. Thick brown hair mixed with gray stuck out of his head an inch all over, and a deep cleft in his chin made a dark shadow beneath his lower lip. The sleeves of his T-shirt were stretched across his biceps, and he wore faded blue jeans that had a job to stay up under his bulging stomach. Huge cowboy boots stuck out at wide angles beneath the cuffs of his jeans.

Dimly she was aware of the small talk, the introductions. She might have been performing on stage for the first time, aware only of the next word, the next movement, the warmth beneath her arms and down her back, the hammering of her heart.

They were looking at her, and she was supposed to answer—with something. "I'm sorry." She gestured futilely. "It's my head. I fell off the dock the day before yesterday, believe it or not. You said something?"

"Only that I'm mighty pleased to be meeting Ron's fiancé."

"Fiancé? I'm sorry. My head. Do you mind if I sit down?"

"Here, let me get you a chair."

Ron said nothing while Ben George scraped an old desk chair across the squeaky boards, but she felt his eyes on her.

"Ron's been telling me about you," Mr. George was saying, "but he didn't tell me you were so pretty."

Ron had said she was pretty? "I'm not anyone's fiancé. And I'm not pretty."

Ben's laugh was the sort that comes from way inside, the kind that can get out only when the head is thrown back.

"Ha!" he roared, plucking the hair along the back of his neck. "Obviously there's a whole lot more Ron didn't tell me about you!"

"I'm sorry," Theresa blustered, catching her breath on her words. She felt the sting of her blush biting her cheeks. "I didn't mean to sound so rude. It's just that, it's just that—" She stopped and looked about the room helplessly. She realized that she was refusing to look at Ron. *How could he?*

"What happened? You say you took a tumble in the drink, Terry?" Ben George was saying. The small boy, Fredrick, had gone to his dad and was wrapped around one blue-jeaned leg. She saw that he stood with both running shoes on top of his dad's left boot.

"It's not Terry, if you don't mind, Mr. George. It's Theresa." Why were people always trying to call her Terry?

"We was showing Theresa around, Dad!" called Fredrick, looking up and tugging on his father's T-shirt. "She used to work here, when it was the Mission. What happened to the trampoline, Dad? She said there was a trampoline—"

"Excuse me, *sir*."

"Excuse me, *sir*," the little boy repeated. "What happened to the trampoline?"

"What trampoline?"

"The one that was in the barn."

"A trampoline in the barn?" Mr. George ruffled his son's hair affectionately. "Where'd you get such a silly notion, boy?"

"Theresa said there was one." The kid swung off his dad's leg.

"Guess we'd better go check that out. Go ahead," he said, redirecting his conversation to Ron. "Take a peek around anywhere you want. You might want to leave the last house on the north side out—that's where we live. I think Leslie is painting. She'll want to have it done right before she lets any company come in. We'll have you over for dinner when she says—okey-doke? Ron, I'll catch you later. Let you folks alone a bit. But Ron, I do want to get those other referrals and references before deciding anything. But it looks A-okay. Just the paperwork to be done. Oh, and I have one more interview. Just formalities, you know how it is. It was nice to meet you, Theresa. Look forward to it again?'' He seemed to wait for a response.

"Yes, yes,'' she mumbled, and then they were gone, and there was just Ron.

"It's good to see you, babe.'' His words were hollow in the sudden quiet of the room. The words bounced in the space. He steered her out the door, hand on her elbow. It seemed to burn a hole through to the bone, but she couldn't pull away; she needed the support.

Then they were outside—out in the front, on the newly raised lawn, passing the bright zinnias and marigolds. Had they moved the flagpole out farther? They must have, when they did the lawns. There were more flags on it too. The Union Jack, the Stars and Stripes, and others—and the good old Maple Leaf, of course.

"Babe, talk to me. Say something,'' Ron was rambling. "I didn't mean for you to find me here. I really didn't. I was going to come and see you, come and talk to you, to beg you to forgive me.''

She pulled away. "You told him we were engaged,'' she said coldly, the words echoing distantly in her ears.

"I did, because we are. We've always—''

"We're not.''

"Well, I mean—''

"What happened to God's will?'' There was a cold knife inside, and it was twisting, making her say things.

"Babe, I'm sorry.''

Babe. When Shawn had tried calling her that, she'd

hollered at him. Oh, Shawn. Ron's presence suddenly seemed offensive.

Shawn? What was she thinking of Shawn for? He was out of her life.

"Do you love me?" Ron asked.

"What?"

"Do you love me?"

"Of course I love you," she said wearily. Where *was* Shawn? Where had he gone? Would he come back?

"Then everything is okay?"

"No. No, it's not. Just because I love you doesn't mean it's okay."

"Tell me what happened to your head." Clearly he didn't want to talk about love anymore.

"I fell off the dock, down at the marina. There was a man who fished me out."

"Well, thank God for that."

"Yes, thank God."

"Can we talk, Theresa? Please?"

"Sure. Talk. No—First, tell me what you're doing here."

"That's what I want to talk about. I came out to—well, to apply for a job with Capernwray. They're looking into the idea—"

He was applying for a job? At Capernwray? At Thetis? It was *her* place. *Her* harbor. No, it wasn't. She didn't have any right.

"Babe? You don't look so good. Are you all right?"

He was going to work at Capernwray. She couldn't shake the thought, the sense of violation. She had come here to get away from him, and now he was going to *work* here.

"Here, let me get you home. You look like you could use a good rest. You're as white as a ghost."

"No, leave me alone. I'm all right."

"No, you're not. There's a bench over here. Let's sit down."

Gratefully she slid into the wrought iron park bench. What was the matter with her, anyway? She felt so weak.

"I'm so sorry," he was saying again. "I guess it was a bit of a shock. I didn't mean to—"

"You told me that already, Ron. Forget it. Just give me a minute and I'll be fine. Guess the inside of my head isn't up to all of this just yet."

Yes, that was it. *Look at all the turmoil I've been in since that whack, she assured herself. Getting charmed by Shawn, fighting with him, storming home, throwing picture and shirt out the back door, then the surprise breakfast and all that cleaning, and the mice—*

"Hey! Wait a minute! Where are you going?" Ron hollered after her, but she kept running. How long had it been? Hours! How many hours had she spent fishing? Two? And the laundry? They'd be dead by the time she got home.

Ron grabbed her arm and yanked hard. "Stop!" he said sternly, snapping her around. "Stop!"

"My mice. They're going to be dead. They're probably already dead."

He shook her arm. "What are you talking about? Never mind, my car is over in the parking lot. You can tell me on the way."

He leaned across the seat and rolled down the windows. The breeze felt good blowing on her forehead. Ron shifted gears and said nothing, waiting for her to talk.

"Well, what are you looking after mice for anyway?" he said at last, impatient with her silence.

"Why? They were all alone, Ron. They would have died." But now they *were* dead. She could see them, curled up around each other, waiting for her, dead in each other's arms. It was all so melodramatic, such a horrible script.

"What do you think the toilet is for?"

"*Ron!*"

"I'm sorry. I'm sorry! I didn't mean it. I'm just kidding, babe." He reached across the car and patted her leg. She pushed his hand away.

"Oh, the laundry," she moaned. "I forgot that too. It's all wrinkled by now."

"I'll take you back to the cabin, then go get it. What dryer were you using?"

"I don't know, Ron."

"Well, what laundry did you do? So I know what to look for."

"The curtains. The yellow curtains. Oh, no! Mr. McCullough's fishing pole! I left it at the wharf."

"I'll get that, too. It'll give me a good excuse to go in and see the old guy. Dad tells me he's been pestering to see me. He look the same?"

"A little balder. Still gives out all-sorts." She leaned back and closed her eyes. The mice were dead and they were discussing how bald Mr. McCullough was. "Can't you hurry?" she asked.

"You want me to drive off the road going around these curves?"

"No."

"Well then, settle down, will you?"

"It just seems to be taking a long time."

"You feeling better now, babe?"

"Better? No, I'm not feeling better."

The mice weren't dead. Yet.

But both of them were motionless, and while Ron warmed the milk, Theresa bundled them each in a bit of the cotton.

"They're not taking it," said Ron, watching her.

"I can see that," she snapped and was immediately sorry. Why was she snapping at him? It was she who was responsible for this. Deftly, she forced a little mouth open and squeezed. The mouse choked. But she kept at it, and finally the milk was gone. She didn't know how much was in their stomachs and how much was all over their fur. The cotton was soaked.

He stood by the back door, waiting. "I'll go get that laundry."

"Thanks, Ron."

"You haven't kissed me yet. I miss your kisses."

"Kiss you? You've got to be kidding."

He shrugged and left with a click to the back door.

"Why should I kiss him?" she whispered to the limp mice, tucking them back into their nest. "Just because he comes back looking sad and trying to be nice?" Shawn's kisses and tender embrace, the way his fingers lingered over her cheek, brushing back her hair, came to haunt her. *Don't think about it,* she told herself for the hundredth time, almost despising the juvenile, sweet-sixteen emotions that played inside.

As it turned out, Ron woke her with a kiss; she'd fallen asleep on the couch.

"You looked so cute," he said, bending over her, and for a minute she was disoriented. What was he doing here, kissing her? Then she remembered and sat up.

"No need to get so huffy," he chided.

"You're not entitled to kiss me," she told him,

fighting hard not to snap at him again. The sun on the water told her it was getting close to supper.

"My, my, you sure can carry a grudge."

"A grudge? A grudge! Oh, my goodness, Ron. Forget it, would you? I don't even want to talk about it. Just go away, please, and leave me alone."

"I brought you your laundry."

"Thanks."

"I want to talk, babe. Please? I want to tell you about this job, about what's been happening to me since I last saw you."

"I don't want to hear it," she said, flopping back down on the chesterfield and burying her face. "Just go away."

"You're so cute, did you know that?"

"What is this?" she demanded, snapping her face clear of the pillows. "Since when have you tried to be charming?"

His attempt at it fell far short of Shawn's charm. Cute. To Shawn she was beautiful. To that George guy, whatever his name was, she was pretty. And to Ron she was *cute*.

Then she reflected. This was the man she had been waiting for for years, the man she had been engaged to. What was she thinking of?

"I'm sorry. I don't know why I'm so grumpy. I'll blame it on my head and lack of sleep. Thanks for getting the laundry."

"You're welcome. I got the fishing pole, too. And I saw Mr. McCullough."

He said it like it was supposed to mean something. She waited. "He's a bit concerned about you," he finally said.

"Ron, if you want to win any Boy Scout points you can hang the curtains back up."

"But they're wrinkled. You'll have to iron them, babe."

"You can win the Eagle award if *you* iron them. And stop calling me *babe*. I'm not your babe." She stood and made her way to the kitchen counter. How long had she been warming milk? It seemed like forever.

"Mr. McCullough is concerned about you," Ron repeated. He flopped in to the armchair in front of the living room windows and tugged on the afghan. It had been there for years, hiding all the holes in the chair. Obviously he had no intention of working on the curtains. Theresa couldn't help seeing a mental picture of Shawn wiping off the table, preparing coffee in the kitchen.

"He said you took quite a spill," Ron was saying. "You didn't tell me it was that serious."

"I'm doing better. You ought to have seen me yesterday. Shawn told me—"

"Shawn?"

"That I looked a mess," she said quickly, stirring the milk as a distraction. Why'd she bring him up?

"The Mr. Malone that Mr. McCullough was telling me about, Theresa?"

She set the spoon down carefully. "So he's lost no time, eh?"

"He's only concerned."

"You know, it's really none of his business. Or yours," she added.

"Says the guy is tall, dark, and handsome. *You* didn't waste much time."

"That is uncalled for!"

"Mr. McCullough tells me this guy apparently makes a habit out of rescuing damsels in distress."

102

"You're being a bully, Ron. You know, I'm feeling a little tired, and it *is* late. So, if you don't mind . . ."

"I'd like to know more about Shawn."

"There's nothing to know. Lock the door on your way out."

"I think you owe me a bit of time, Theresa. I did, after all, track down your fishing pole and laundry."

He was doing it again—making her feel as though *she* were in the wrong, rather than he. Already he'd gotten her to apologize for being grumpy when he was the one who kept at her, as if being a gentleman entitled him to be a pest.

"You like him, Theresa?" he asked, pushing her, poking her with his questions.

"For Pete's sake, I only met him two days ago!"

"What do you know about him?"

"This conversation is getting a little out of hand, don't you think?"

"What do you know about him?"

Before she used to answer all these questions, as though she didn't have a choice. Standing here now, stirring warm milk, hearing tiny mouse squeaks in the background, seeing Ron pick at the afghan, she suddenly realized she didn't have to answer anything she didn't want to. Then suddenly she *wanted* to answer him.

"You want to know about Shawn Malone?" she asked. "Well, I'll tell you. Mr. McCullough is right. Shawn Malone is tall, dark, and handsome. He's charming and witty and has the most amazing dimple you ever saw. He used to be a Young Life leader in Seattle. Now let me think. What else do I know? What else is there to know about Shawn Malone? I guess nothing. That's probably it, Ron. I guess that's all I know."

"Being a snot doesn't become you, Theresa."

"So I'm a snot now, am I? First you were implying that I was a tramp. And now I'm a snot." They were fighting just like when they were kids.

"I'm worried about you, Theresa."

"Don't bother. I'm a big girl."

"Well, Mr. McCullough seems to think you're rather enraptured by the man. And you really don't know anything about him, do you?"

"I know he's not a rat like you."

He let it pass. "And yet you spent an entire afternoon below deck with him. You let him cook you steak on that boat of his. And you looked like the world had come to an end when he disappeared overnight."

"Mr. McCullough's been *real* busy."

"Oh, come off it. He's concerned, that's all."

"Shawn fished me out of the water, and we became friends," she said, trying to bring some reasonableness back to the conversation. "He seems very nice. And yes, I like him. And I don't care to discuss it with you anymore."

The mice didn't look any better. Gently she prodded open their mouths, her worry seeping in. "Ron? Do you think they'll be all right?"

He bent over to take a peek. "They don't look good, do they? Did you look for their mother at all?"

"Saw a mouse on the porch yesterday. Could have been her."

What was the matter with her, anyway? That she could be so mad at Ron one minute and so dependent upon him for support the next. He unlocked the front door and went out to check the porch.

I really do love him, she realized, although not in

the old way anymore. His coming to the island had made her realize that, along with the memory of Shawn's kisses, her perspective had changed a great deal in the last couple of days. Why had she spent so much time being sick over this?

"Ron," she called in a quiet voice.

He came to the door. "Yes?"

"I really am sorry."

The sun glanced off his blond hair, shimmering it with golden lights. His eyes were especially blue.

"About what, babe?"

"About everything. About us. You and me. I'm sorry about the squabbling. About snapping at you. About not wanting to talk to you about what's on your mind. I guess I really don't want to hear it. I'm not up to it, I guess. I know I haven't reacted very well, even though, well, you're trying so hard—" She stopped. Now it was she who was rambling.

"You like this guy, don't you?"

The water reflected the blue sky. A small boat buzzed by, leaving behind a small wake that disappeared with the sound.

"You love him."

Theresa bit her lip so the pain could clear her head.

"*You do, don't you?*"

"I think—" She hurt all over.

"It's all right. Just tell me. I can take it."

"Ron, I really do love you. It's just that. . . . "

"It's just that what?"

She sensed him bristling and she stared at the lost wake from the boat. Where had it gone? Washed up on the beach as if it had never been? Was that what was coming of her and Ron, too—a ripple in the water, and then no more? How could she just let that happen?

"Babe, answer me."

"I'm not your babe!" she cried, breaking suddenly free from her thoughts. "You threw me out, remember? You told me it was all God's will. You told me we loved each other out of some sick sense of need. You told me a bunch of lies because you *really* thought some other woman looked a whole lot better. It wasn't God at all, you big creep! You jilted me! So what are you here now for? Did she jilt *you?*"

There was a terrible silence. Ron licked his lips and looked at her helplessly. She might as well have slapped him.

"Oh, Ron, I'm sorry. I didn't mean—"

"You love Shawn, don't you?"

"I didn't say that."

"You're not denying it, I noticed."

"Maybe you'd better leave."

"I was a fool. I—"

"You weren't honest with me, Ron."

"I know. And I'm sorry."

She should say something, but she couldn't think of a thing. Even his being sorry didn't make a difference, somehow. He backed out the door and was gone.

"Ron!" she cried, running after him. And then she was in his arms, crying as if her heart would break— except it had already broken. He stroked her hair and held her tight and she whispered over and over, "I'm sorry, Ron. I'm sorry. I wish we could go back, but we can't."

And when he left she knew it was the way it had to be.

CHAPTER 8

IT WAS SO QUIET. And night was coming on.

Now what do I do? Theresa wondered. Feelings and thoughts jumped around in her head, making her restless. But the ache she felt for Ron sapped the energy she needed to light a fire. So she sat bundled in a blanket, staring out the dark window. It was over. It was really over now. Like a light going out. And there were no tears—which was a relief. She felt empty inside.

After a bit the cold got to her and she stirred. She'd missed supper again. Not that she felt like eating anything. She scrubbed her face, brushed her teeth, and slipped into her orange flannel nightie, the one that said *If Only I had a Brain*.

I ought to have gotten the tinman one, she thought. *I need a heart. What am I saying? I have a heart. It just got broken, is all.*

Words like *broken* and *over* and *the end* played with each other in her mind. Half an hour ago she'd felt sorry that Ron felt so bad, sorry it had to end so dismally, sorry she'd hollered. But now that the sorry had worked its way through, there was only a strange emptiness that didn't feel particularly good. *Maybe I don't have a heart. I don't feel anymore.*

But she knew that wasn't true. She was feeling a lot of things. There were a lot of emotions flitting in and out inside her head. And while smearing a knife full of peanut butter across a slice of bread, she named it. *Shawn.* With Ron out of the way for sure, Shawn loomed larger than life in the small cabin.

Tall, dark, handsome Shawn—the stranger who had a habit of rescuing damsels in distress. Shawn, who kissed like a Harlequin hero and teased and charmed like a movie star—or, at least, as she imagined Harlequin heroes might kiss and movie stars might tease and charm.

But Shawn had sailed out of her life and there was no point in thinking about him. Even so, the nagging feeling persisted, and so did the image of the dimple in his cheek.

This was silly. What time was it, anyway? Ten o'clock.

She put the tea kettle on, read through her journal a bit, walked around the cabin, folded the laundry, felt guilty about the story that she hadn't begun working on. Had Ron gone back to Capernwray? It was odd to think of the old place as Capernwray. And where was Shawn? Where had he gone? And how many times had she asked herself that question?

"What is wrong with me?" she finally exploded aloud, exasperated. Did she really love him? Was Ron right?

That was ridiculous. She hardly knew Shawn—

other than that he used to be a Young Life leader and hated fanatics. So what was it she felt?

Excitement. Thrill. Quivers of electricity and spice down her backbone. He was the knight in shining armor, a storybook character come to life. It appealed to her writer's imagination. But was that all he was? King Arthur?

Find a good book and climb into bed, she told herself. *Get a good night's sleep and you'll have it all figured out by morning.*

But she couldn't find a good book and she couldn't fall asleep. Once she had seen a game show in which Paul Lynde had been asked, "What does Billy Graham do when he can't get to sleep?" Paul Lynde had laughed and answered like a smart-alec, "He reads the Bible." Turned out, that's exactly what B. G. did, so Theresa turned on the lamp, found the zippered Bible, and fluffed up the pillows behind her back. Much later she was startled by the alarm clock reminding her to feed the mice.

They still weren't responding and she held back tears of frustration and guilt while patiently prodding their mouths open, coaxing them to swallow. "Come on," she whispered.

There was a knock on the door.

"Yes?" She called from the couch.

"It's Shawn. Can I come in?"

"Shawn?" In one bound, Theresa was out of the couch, both mice clutched in her hand. "Oh, Shawn!" she cried, then stopped, embarrassed. Then, in a calmer voice, "Come in."

"Hello. Was in the neighborhood. Thought I'd drop in and see if you—" He gave her an easy hug. "Mmm. You smell good."

"Thank you," she choked, standing helpless in her bathrobe, still holding the mice. He kissed the top of her head as though it were the most logical thing to do. "Well, well, what is it we have here?"

"Shawn, I thought I'd never see you again!" she cried in spite of herself, staring up into his wonderful face. It was just as she remembered it. He smiled and her heart fluttered. Then he chucked her chin, the way they did in the movies, and kissed her.

"It's only been a day or two," he said. That was just a line in a book, too; apparently she wasn't going to get any more out of him. Obviously he wasn't used to explaining himself to anyone.

"Tell me about these mice," he said. "Hey, what's *this*?" He stood back, one side of his mouth turning up, then the other, till finally his lips opened and revealed his straight white teeth in a grin.

Theresa looked down self-consciously where her bathrobe had parted a little. "Are you laughing at my nightie?"

"No." But then he burst out laughing.

"You *are* laughing at my nightie." She pulled the sash more tightly around her waist.

"*If only I had a brain?*"

"Try to put up with it, Mr. Malone. It's warm and does the job."

He laughed. "The bump on your head is looking pretty good."

"It's doing okay. Where have you been?"

"What have you got here? Let me see," he said, glancing at her, then laughing again. He settled into the chesterfield and tugged her down beside him. "Where'd you get them?" He stroked a finger over the small bodies still clutched in her hand.

"Where have you been?"

But he ignored her again. "Where'd you get these?"

"My uncle's bathrobe pocket."

He took them carefully and held them up for inspection, and Theresa found herself telling him the whole story. But all the while she wondered why, when all she wanted to know was where he had been, why he was back, and what was he going to do.

"Where's the mother?" he asked when she was all done.

"I don't know. Scurried out the back hole."

"Where's the Monterey Jack I left the other day?"

"In the fridge. Why?"

"Where's the hole?"

"In the bathroom, under the dresser."

She followed him as he sliced off a chuck of the cheese, then knelt on the bathroom floor to find the hole.

"I'll tell you what we're going to do," he said, pushing the cheese close to the back wall and spreading crumbs across the floor to just under the sink.

We? Did she hear him right?

"We're going to hang your little babies back on the door—your uncle mind if we lower the nail?—and between feedings we'll put them back where the mother knows they last were, and maybe, just maybe she'll return and take over. We'll keep feeding them until then."

We?

"Come on. You look like you're in a state of shock."

"I am."

111

"When's the last time you fed these little critters?" he asked, stroking them gently. He rubbed their heads between the miniature ears. "You go climb into bed. I'll take over. You look like you could get some rest."

"I won't be able to sleep."

"Go on. You look exhausted."

"I won't be able to go to sleep while you're here. I mean—"

"You slept well enough the last time I was here," he teased.

"I didn't know you were here then."

He regarded her carefully.

"Where have you been?" she asked again, realizing it was the third or fourth time, and the third of fourth time he'd ignored her.

"Tell me, when do these things need to be fed again, and how often?"

"Shawn!"

"How often?"

"Every two hours. Shawn where have you been? What were you doing? How come you're back? And how come you're at Thetis in the first place, anyway?"

"Such a lot of questions for so late at night. When did you say was the last time you fed these things?"

"Shawn!"

"When?"

"I was feeding them when you came in."

"What are you feeding them?"

"Milk."

"Still warm?"

"Probably."

"Then show me what to do."

She tested the milk, filled the eyedropper, and

handed it over. "You have to force their mouths open and pray they don't choke when you squeeze."

"Father, be with these little critters—"

"What are you doing?" she asked in surprise as he pried one mouth open gently.

His eyes danced in the warm glow of the dark cabin. "You said to pray."

"Well, for heaven's sake, I didn't mean—"

"Hey, look at this little one." The mouse had gagged, but now it was rubbing its face with a paw.

"You were praying over a *mouse*?"

"You told me to, love."

Love? "Shawn, you were praying over a *mouse*. A *mouse*, Shawn!"

"Tsk, tsk. A minute ago you were blubbering over these mice, and now you're—"

"What's gotten into you?" He was teasing her, deliberately goading her, making fun.

"Hey, look. This little guy is really getting the hang of it! Look at him."

"Shawn!"

"You think praying over cold eggs is more justifiable than praying over a couple of starving mice, Theresa?"

"Shawn!" she cried, exasperated beyond belief. "Don't tease!"

"So it is, is it?" His cheeks nearly buried his eyes, so big was his smile.

"Shawn!" Lunging for him, she pummeled him with both fists. His eyes sparkled with the fun he was having. "What's gotten into you, anyway? You're being awfully mean!"

"Hey, watch it!" Arm over his head, he pulled loose and stood, towering above her. "You're going to make me drop these babies!"

113

She went and sat in the chair with the afghan, opposite the sofa. She picked at the threads until she remembered Ron had been doing that, then she yanked her hand back. Staring at Shawn, she waited for him to say something.

He didn't. He just sat quietly, poking the eyedropper into his fist. She couldn't see the mice, but he seemed to be doing it right.

"Are they eating?" she finally asked.

"Mmm. One is asleep. Is there a hammer around here?"

"In the bathroom."

"Here, take them a minute, will you? I'm going to fix that nail. I'll be back. Don't go away." He leaned over and kissed her.

She smiled in surprise, then watched him saunter through the cabin. She could hear him banging about in the bathroom. How could everything be so absolutely dreamy all of a sudden? Doris Day and the whole business.

"There, that's done. Here, give me these little guys." He took them from her, and when he returned, their eyes met. He smiled slowly. "May I stay a bit?"

She nodded, afraid to say yes.

They talked late into the night. Shawn built a fire, then later put on a pot of tea. Sometimes he rose to stare into the dark night, and in those comfortable, silent times came the sound of the sea lapping the beach below.

Theresa memorized his face, the way it moved when he said things, the way he tilted his head to emphasize certain points. They talked of the weather, of Thetis, of the ferry system. They laughed and joked, and once they sat with nothing to say until it got too strained.

It was Shawn who broke the silence. "I've been sailing up and down the Straight. You triggered a lot of things in me, you know, Theresa." He smiled and glanced at her quickly. "So I've been out trying to put God in His place, if you want to know the truth." It was a sudden switch in the conversation, but Theresa was getting used to his switches.

"It seems He's been putting me in mine, though," Shawn went on. He'd planted himself in front of the dark windows again, feet spread, hands tucked into his back pockets. "You want to know why I called you a fanatic?"

"Because I prayed over cold eggs."

"Because you reminded me of someone."

"Oh." She didn't like the sound of it.

"Someone I loved," he said, and she caught her breath on the past tense. "When she died I told God to go jump. Anyone who bothered with God I stuck in the fanatic category, that way I could excuse myself from the active duty list."

She watched his somber reflection in the window.

"Her name was Julie," he went on. "She was a good, sweet woman. I met her at the University of Washington. She was a med student. Smarter than anyone I knew. And she loved people. Life. Me. More than anything else, she loved God. But she died."

The reflection in the glass showed a bottom lip caught between white teeth, eyes that looked far past the night to time past.

"I'm sorry," she whispered, as the ghosts of her own family crept in. For some reason she could see her grandfather, seated at the table on Fraser Street, serviette tucked into his neck and eating corn on the cob, passing her the salt and pepper.

"Hodgkins disease. She never told me she'd had it as a teenager. She was in remission."

His pain was raw, and it seemed to bleed into the room. He was carrying his pain around as she was.

"The last time I saw her she had tubes down her nose, hoses into her throat. Needles jabbed the skin in her temples and arms. Catheters stretched from under the bedsheets. A machine sucked air in and out of her lungs. Her hair, Theresa, was greasy and wet. She was a tortured ghost."

"My grandpa died of cancer."

"I know. You told me. You know, when Julie died, I died. And I hated God. I hated him for doing this— not for taking away from me the person I loved, but because she deserved better than what she got. It seemed to me at the time that God had a funny way of thanking His help."

It was remarkable how they were questioning some of the same things at the same time. Shawn tossed a pillow off the chesterfield and flopped down across from her.

"You know something?" he said, swinging his feet over the end. "When I first saw you, splashing around and crying out for your Ron, it was like a dying root way inside of me had found water." He sighed and grinned. Firelight caught in his eyes. "For the first time I felt alive. Really alive. Can I tell you how exciting it was to dive in after you? To rescue something? Someone?" He half sat. "To laugh death in the face and drag its next victim out of its very jaws? Can I tell you the raw thrill of my defiance?"

The intensity of his feelings surprised her. "No, I suppose not," he went on. "You see, I cheated death. It doesn't win all the time."

"In the end it does," she said, remembering her folks. Grandpa.

Shawn threw his legs to the floor and paced. "You're wrong, you know. You're wrong. What's that verse, 'Death, where is thy sting?' I've learned something. In the end death doesn't win. God does."

"Is this the same Shawn talking?" she teased. He ignored her and barreled on.

"Theresa, my last image of Julie was a tortured ghost. It's haunted me every day of my life since then. But two days ago I got a new look." He went to the window again. "'For now we see in a mirror dimly, but then face to face. Now I know in part; then I shall understand fully.'"

"You had to memorize Scripture when you were a kid, too, I see."

His reflection in the glass smiled at her. "Two days ago, when I fished you out of the water, that mirror didn't seem quite so dim. The ghost faded, like dust on a dirty window when you go at it with window cleaner. I saw Julie whole again, pulled free of that ghost costume."

He spoke to Theresa through the dark window. "When I held you in my lap, dripping wet, I got a sense of what it must be like to be God. The power He must have over death. When Julie died, God fished her out of the sea, so to speak. When she died, He must have held her just as I held you. The tortured ghost image faded while I sat with you in my lap waiting for that doctor to arrive. While you lived and breathed, I knew Julie lived and breathed, too. She wasn't a ghost anymore. It was as if the whole horrible masquerade party was over, and God wasn't the villain anymore. No more Dracula, preying on pretty maidens.''

"You've got a graphic imagination.''

"So do you. I love the way you think. You think like me, you know.''

"Can I ask you something?''

"Sure.''

"If God quit being Dracula that day, how come you were so angry with me that night? Calling me a fanatic and everything—you know, the Sara-Lee-Banana-Cake routine.''

He turned to face her directly. "Because it scared me. With the charade over, who was I? Who was God? I mean, all those years, holding onto my sense of injustice. And then in one instant it was over and I realized my own blindness. What do you do when the mask falls off? You try to put it back on. It makes you feel safe—even if it makes you angry. Besides,'' he added, "I was smitten with you and you rejected me.''

She swallowed and blinked and knew she must look terribly foolish. The old shivers skittered up her back and she trembled under his gaze. She could look into his eyes forever.

"Did you ever see 'Sound of Music'?'' he asked, closing the space between them in long strides.

She took a sharp breath and unconsciously tightened the afghan under her neck. "Seven times,'' she whispered, unable to let go of his eyes.

He knelt in front of her. "Remember when Christopher Plummer and Julie Andrews were out in the garden and he told her he'd fallen in love with her when she sat on 'that ridiculous pinecone'?''

"And she fell in love with him when he blew that 'silly whistle'?"

"I fell in love with you the minute I heard you calling out for your ridiculous Ron."

She felt her lips doing strange things. Her mouth was dry. He was in love with her. The words bounced around and gave her a heady sensation.

"I know, I know. It sounds crazy, but I swear, sitting on that dock, holding you, waiting for the doctor, I fell in love with you. It was as if I suddenly woke up from a bad dream. What's crazier is that I blamed God for that, too. Can you believe it?"

He was in love with her. He said he loved her. She focused on the dimple in his cheek.

"You talked about your grandpa dying. And your folks. And Ron jilting you. But you're so very alive. Full of fun and spit. And when I saw the way you handled Mr. McCullough, why, that was a prize—I'd love to live that all over again." He stopped to chuckle and remember. "You didn't know I was listening to all that, did you?"

"You were supposed to be buying meat."

"A talent of mine. I can do things at the same time." He grinned and hesitantly she held out her hand. He caught it and put it to his face. His cheek was warm.

Silence descended into the air like a blanket on a cold night. Still he knelt before her. "You are so alive, Theresa, and you've had so much worse happen to you. And then you prayed over those stupid eggs! That was the last straw."

"It was more a habit than honest gratitude," she said, smiling at him. She pulled away her hand. "But you're wrong about my being so alive, you know."

"How so?"

"The last few weeks I've been walking around more dead than alive." His eyes were kind and soft. She suppressed a desire to touch him again, concentrating instead on what she was saying. "Oh, maybe going through the motions, but really I was dead inside. That's why I came out here, you know, to find some sort of peace."

"You could have fooled me. You seemed to have it licked, tossing your head and declaring your Ron a nobody."

She couldn't help but smile. "Maybe I fooled myself, too. But the last couple of days have been like—you know how it is when you sit on your leg too long and it goes to sleep?"

"Mmm."

"The last couple of days have been like that. Like the pins and needles you get when you finally stand up. No, maybe it's more like frostbite thawing." She remembered the walk home in the shadows last night, feeling so alone. "Sometimes it's been really hard. I've been feeling abandoned."

"Come here," he said, rising and taking her hand. "Abandon this old stuffy chair and come sit with me on the couch—or is it *chesterfield* up here?"

"It's chesterfield."

He led her across the room and pulled her down next to him. Shyly she snuggled close, fitting under his arm as if it were made for her. They didn't speak for several minutes. He ran his hand up and down her arm. It was warm and assuring, and at the same time exciting.

"Did you feel abandoned when Julie died?" she asked at last, looking up into his handsome face.

"Abandoned? That's a strange word. But yes, now that I think about it, I guess I did."

"I've discovered that abandonment is a favorite feeling of mine. Doesn't seem to matter what happens, I feel left behind."

"That's understandable." His arm tightened about her. "Getting dumped by what's-his-face didn't help, I'm sure."

"You know what I figured out, though? I don't think you can abandon an adult. A baby, yes, but not an adult. An adult can always pick up the pieces and go on."

He nuzzled her ear and smoothed back a few loose hairs. *This is amazing,* she thought, *sitting here in the wee hours, pouring out my soul to this man, who is still very much a stranger.*

"I like the way you think," he whispered. He turned her face to meet his. His eyes darted back and forth as he looked at her.

"Can I show you something in the Bible," she asked, a little afraid.

His dimple flashed. "You act as though it might make me mad or something."

"Well, . . ."

He grinned. "I guess I deserved that."

"I want to show you a verse that my uncle and aunt—" She stopped. "Remember the picture?"

"Picture?"

"Of Ron."

"Oh! The one you threw at me!"

"The one with the instructions to buried treasure on the back."

"So you found some sort of treasure?" His eyes were round and dark and full of mischief again.

"My uncle had a Bible reference in the postscript to a note he gave me. It's sort of like a treasure, I guess."

Shawn didn't laugh. He was waiting for her to go on.

"You want to look it up?" she asked.

"Sure. Where is your old Bible?"

She slid off the couch and dropped the Bible into his lap. "Psalm 56:8. I need to get something in the kitchen."

She came back with the agates and sat down beside him while he read out loud: "Thou hast kept count of my tossings; put thou my tears in thy bottle!"

"My aunt collects these," she said, handing him the glass jar. "For some reason I get this silly vision of Chehalis milk bottles lining God's windowsills."

He grinned. "You see? I *like* the way you think. You've got a super imagination." He poured a few of the smooth stones into his palm. The light of the fire made them look dark and heavy, but when he held one up, the clearness came, and all the bright color.

"You know," he said, "sometimes they call agates Apache tears."

She wriggled under his arm again, as though she'd been doing it for years, and they sat under the warm blanket of silence. The dying fire hissed once in a while. An ember threw off a spark. Theresa, sleepy and happy beyond words, marveled that God had turned everything around so suddenly.

Then she felt Shawn lift her off the couch and carry her into the bedroom. "It's time for you to go to bed," he whispered when she opened her eyes.

"What about the mice?" she mumbled.

"I told you. I'll take care of them." He pushed the bedroom door open with his shoulder.

"Are you sure?" She knew she was ignoring her real feelings again, although her heart pounded wildly.

"Of course I am."

"Shawn?"

"Yes?" He held her in his arms still, looking down into her face.

"Are you sure you're in love with me?"

He nodded gravely. "Why?"

She slid her arms around his neck. "Because I think I might be falling in love with you."

He smiled so slowly, then lowered her into the bed. He tucked the covers up as if she were a kid.

"I'm afraid to kiss you," he confessed. "So I'm not going to, okay?"

"Okay."

"I'll be right outside. If you need anything, just let me know, okay?"

"Okay."

He paused a moment before closing the door. The light spilled in. He was a tall, dark shape.

"Shawn?"

"Yes?"

"Where's Bear?"

"On the boat."

"Doesn't he get lonely?"

"Don't worry about it, love."

"Okay."

The door shut and she fell asleep dreaming of the kiss he hadn't given her.

CHAPTER 9

OVERNIGHT THE CLOUDS SNEAKED in and Theresa woke to dampness and the sound of raindrops hitting the tin roof. *What a gloomy day*, she thought. Then she remembered Shawn.

Memories of the night before rolled in, of all that had been said between them. Theresa sifted through it lazily, enjoying it, savoring it. She stared at the ceiling, going through all the delicious times, until she came to the part when she'd told him sleepily that she thought she might be falling in love with him.

Now why did I do that? she moaned, the lazy explorations fleeing as energy rode in on a wave of adrenalin. This morning it all seemed a bit unreal.

Well, do I? she demanded of herself, not letting the memory go. He loved her. No, he *said* he loved her. But how could he? He didn't really know her.

But he did love her. She knew he did. It was in his eyes, in the way he spoke to her. She'd never felt so loved before. It was as though up until now *nobody* had loved her, although she knew that wasn't true.

But did she love him? She didn't know. How could she know? *I must be sensible about this*, she thought. After all, it *had* been only a few days. Time works things out, and I have nearly five weeks to know my mind.

That put to rest, sheer energy propelled her from the bed. Cracking the newly hung, faded yellow priscillas, complete with wrinkles, she looked out to a gray world. All around, everywhere she looked, it was gray on gray, with white froth on gray sea. Shawn's boat, moored fifty yards out, rose and sank on the gray swell. For some reason she hadn't thought he'd be anchored offshore. She had assumed he had the boat safely moored at the marina.

"Shawn?" she called out. "Maybe you'd better get your boat down to the marina. Shawn?"

There was no answer. For a moment she was frightened, the old sense of abandonment rushing in. He'd run off, he'd left her. Jilted again. But the boat sitting out on the water defied her fright.

"What a silly," she mumbled, then realized he must be sleeping and immediately regretted having called. He'd been feeding the mice all night; he had to be exhausted.

She dressed methodically, pulling on warm cords and a blue sweatshirt with white sailboats silk-screened across the chest. Pulling the collar of her blouse out over the neck of the sweatshirt, and adjusting the blouse sleeves so that they just barely peeked out, Theresa sat on the bed and tugged on her socks. Today was not a day for sandals or running shoes. It was a day for wool socks and gum boots.

How many days had she awakened to skies like this, and dressed for this kind of day, sitting on this very bed, pulling on thick socks, wondering if any-body else was up yet?

Ron used to love days like this. Long before any of them had been awake, he'd have headed on down the beach, catching the splash of waves on his pantlegs. He wouldn't come home until he was soaked and his restlessness driven from him.

Glancing out the window, she half-expected to see Ron hiking along the rocks below the cliff. Something inside called out to him. It was over, but she realized she had a residue of love left. She wanted to hang onto it, to cultivate it, to somehow work things out. But did such things happen? She didn't know.

"It *is* a gloomy day," she said.

The cabin was warm when she opened the bedroom door. Shawn must have stirred up the fire at some point, but other than an occasional crackle, there was no other sound. Outside, the wind rushed the corners of the house, and below, the surf crashed into the rocks. Theresa tiptoed across the kitchen floor and into the bathroom. She washed her face, brushed her hair, (remembering the other morning when Shawn had demanded that she brush it), checked her fore-head, and looked in on the mice.

To her surprise, there was the mother, big and fat and feeding the two babies. "Oh, thank you, God," she whispered, then realized with embarrassment that it was *she* who was praying over the mice now. She was glad Shawn was still asleep and couldn't hear.

When she had the tea kettle going and two pieces of toast buttered, still there was no stir from the living room. *The poor man*, she thought, and took a peek.

The blankets were folded neatly over the end of the empty chesterfield. He was gone!

"He went for a walk," she said aloud, taking a deep breath and double-checking out the window. The boat was still there. Donning a rainjacket and a warm toque, she hurried outside, gasping involuntarily at the roar of the wind. It whipped her hair into her eyes. She bent into the wind and tugged on the toque frantically to bring it over her ears.

Then she spotted him sitting atop a large boulder on the beach, arms folded around his drawn-up knees.

"Shawn!" she shouted. The wind took her words. "*Shawn!*"

He turned and waved.

"What are you doing?" she hollered, trying to out-holler the wind. But it was futile. So she scurried down the slippery cliff, being careful not to do it somersault-style.

"What are you doing?" she yelled again as she neared him. "You're going to catch your death!"

"Oh, but I love it!" He sat bare headed, the wind playing havoc with his hair. His cheeks were bitten with red, and he seemed to glory in the raw elements of the growing storm. "Come on up!"

"How?"

"Here, take a hand!"

Clawing and scrambling, crunching barnacles under her boots, getting soaked clean through, she clambered up beside him. Once she slipped, but he grabbed her arm and held her steady.

"Thank you," she whispered, suddenly shy, caught in the wondering of his eyes. They were full of questions.

"Mama Mouse came back," she said, and sat awkwardly on the cold, wet rock beside him. He slipped an arm around her. The water heaved and broke and splattered the beach. Far off, past the other islands nearby, was the open Georgia Straight. Due east was the mouth of the Fraser River, where the fishermen sat in dots of boats on drizzly days during the salmon run.

"Don't you love weather like this?" Shawn asked. He was blocking the worst of the wind, although the rain fell steadily, driving against her pantlegs. "Just feel it! Doesn't that wind just talk to you?"

"But it's so gloomy!"

"Nonsense! It's all in the way you look at it."

She thought about it for a moment. To her it was gloomy. To Ron, she realized, it was soothing. To Shawn it was exhilarating.

"Hear it?" he demanded. "Do you hear it talk? Just look! The sea, the almighty sea, is at the wind's mercy! Doesn't it seem to say that everything has its time?"

Yes, the wind did seem to talk. It whistled and bent the trees and beat the waves until whitecaps rode the peaks. It tugged the words from Shawn's mouth, too, and flung them down the beach, but the truth of them lingered. Everything had its time. Yes, she could hear it, too.

"What do you have to do today?" he asked suddenly.

"Work, I guess. Why?"

"Just wondered if you would mind my spending the day."

Spend the whole day? With her!

"I had an appointment to keep," he was saying, "but with this weather, I haven't the interest to stir myself. You have a phone in that cabin?"

There were so many things she wanted to ask him.

Like, What do you do for a living? How is it you have this marvelous boat? Where is your appointment, and what is it about? She wanted to know everything about him.

"Do you have a phone?" he asked again.

"Yes."

"May I stay? Or am I interrupting something?"

"Oh, sure. I mean, no." What a dither she was in, just contemplating having him around! "I mean, sure you can stay. And no, you're not interrupting anything. I was just going to do a bit of writing."

"You *write*?"

She was sensitive about her writing. Most people seemed to think it was something of a pipedream—everyone, that is, but her uncle. She shrugged nonchalantly, wary of Shawn's reaction. "A bit."

"Published?"

"Just high school stuff."

"Just high school stuff! Listen to this woman." He sat up and took a closer look at her. Rain ran off his face.

"My professor at U-Dub thinks I ought to write a book," she ventured, sensing genuine interest.

"What professor?"

"Dr. Sorenson. But I don't know. I just can't see myself doing it. I'm more comfortable with short stories—"

"Dr. Sorenson? *The* Dr. Sorenson?"

"You know him?"

"Of course I know him—took classes from him. And if he thinks you ought to write a book, Theresa, then how come you're not writing a book?"

"Wait a minute. Back up a bit, Shawn Malone. Why did you take classes from Dr. Sorenson?"

129

His grin was about as big as they come.

"What's so funny?" she demanded, getting defensive, feeling the bristle up her back. "Quit laughing! Or I won't let you stay. I'll send you off in the middle of the storm and I'll—"

"And you'll what?"

"Oh, I don't know what! Quit laughing, will you?"

"Oh, Theresa, I can't believe it. No wonder I like the way you think. You've got a writer's mind. I can't believe it."

"Can't believe what?"

"That you're really a writer!"

"And what's so unbelievable about that?" she demanded.

"Nothing. Nothing at all. I'm just jealous, is all."

"Jealous?"

"Do you know how long it took me to get published?"

Puzzle pieces fell out of a box. "Whoa. . . . " Rain streamed down the back of her neck while she fiddled with a loose strip of rubber along the top of her left gum boot. What had her uncle said? Maybe there was somebody else for her, somebody more like her?

"Don't tell me you're a writer," she said, hardly daring to breathe.

"'Fraid so."

"And you took classes from my professor," she continued, putting the pieces together one at a time.

"I got my master's in fiction under him."

"And you sail around in that boat of yours and you write stories."

He nodded while she spoke.

"And I suppose that's what you're doing up here— working on another story." The puzzle pieces had come together in a pretty startling way. Just the wonder of it left her breathless. She was falling in love with a writer, an honest-to-goodness writer at that.

Shawn's hands closed over hers and stopped her game with the gum boot. She was afraid to look at him, so she stared at his hands covering hers.

"Last week," he said, running his fingers over the backs of her hands. "I would have said Fate. But today I'm not sure. It all seems ordained somehow, doesn't it?"

"What a fancy word," she said, still going over the pieces. "Ordained." She pulled the wet hair out from under her collar. "What have you written? Do you write stories or books? Nonfiction? No, you said fiction."

"Yes, fiction."

Shawn Malone. Whipping through the memory tracks, she sought to match title with author. Shawn Malone, Shawn Malone. . . .

She stared at him.

"'Fraid so," he said.

"I don't believe it. You wrote *Not from the Beginning*?"

"Mm—m."

"*Doctor, Lawyer, Indian Chief*?"

"Mm—m."

"*Cedar Boy*?"

"Mm—m."

Goodness. She sat back to catch her breath. Here she was, Theresa Parker, dabbling writer, sitting right next to one of the best. She stole a quick look, then picked at her boot again. He was watching her. She tugged on the loose piece of rubber. He'd kissed her. Told her he was in love with her. And said he was jealous. Of her! It was enough to make her head whirl, though of course he was teasing.

"I just don't believe it," she muttered, flinging the rubber piece over the rock. "I'm so embarrassed!" Raising one knee and resting her chin on her wet pantleg, she stared out to the churning sea.

"Embarrassed?" He laughed loudly and pulled her close with both arms so that she lost her balance. She fell against his side, catching his kiss as she slid toward him. "Tell me, why are you embarrassed?"

"You're the author of six absolutely marvelous books!" she said, tipping her head back into his arm. "And I was ready to believe you when you said you were jealous of me. Me. *I'm* jealous!" Playfully she punched his leg.

"Aha!" he exclaimed, grabbing her wrist. "But look who started publishing first? You! In high school, yet."

"But nothing since then," she reminded him.

He shook his head. "How hard have you tried?"

"I haven't."

"Well, that's your problem. You've got to get going." He sat her up. "Dr. Sorenson said he thought you ought to do a book?" She nodded. "Then what are you waiting for?"

"I guess I'm trying to think of one."

"Think of one! *Think of one?* That's your problem. You don't *think* of them, honey. You look around you and *find* them! And then you start writing them, and they—" He stopped in midstream. "What's the matter?"

"You called me honey."

"Well, of course I did."

"It sounded, it sounded kind of nice." Now why did she feel like crying all of a sudden?

"Oh, Theresa," whispered Shawn, pulling her to his lap. He kissed her long and hard while the rain washed their skin.

"Shawn," she murmured. There was a glory in being in his arms, God's rain beating down upon them, his face close to hers, kissing her, talking to her, touching her cheek with his hand.

"I *love* you," he whispered, holding her close. "You remember my telling you that last night?"

Heart pounding, she nodded, caught up this time in both his telling her and his showing her. She received his kisses and gave them back, wondering if ever she had been so happy. Searching her mind, she couldn't remember a time anything had seemed so right, so wonderful.

"Do you love *me*?" he asked, kissing each of her eyes, then holding her face, catching her eyes with his own. "Say yes," he whispered, his lips moving, the wind muffling his words. He cupped her face in his hands. "Say yes," he said again, not letting her go.

Joy lurched against apprehension and collided in her stomach and she went cold with the fright of what was coming.

"Please say yes," he teased, kissing her again, kissing her eyes, her cheeks, tipping her head to kiss her ears. The fright dissolved under his touch like ice cubes dropped into hot chocolate. The cold turned to warmth. Joy melted the fright, drowned away the last of apprehension, and she knew without a shadow of doubt. God's signature was set in the lower righthand corner of this jigsaw puzzle; it was that perfect.

"Oh, Shawn—"

"Wait, I don't want to hear it yet," he whispered, sliding his hands over her face and into her wet hair, knocking off her toque. He lifted her face to meet his. "Just let me finish kissing you before you tell me to get lost."

The joy of loving him burst loose like a river and she threw her arms about him, captured heart and soul by this audacious, fun-loving, kind, and gentle man God had brought into her life.

"Do I take it this means you do?"

She started to laugh and slapped a hand to her mouth, laughing at him with her eyes.

"You do, don't you?"

She nodded, and his kiss was slow and gentle this time, like the touch of a feather.

"Oh, Shawn," she murmured. "Ron said that one day I'd thank him for dumping me. I think that day just happened."

"It's not Fate, is it? I think we can really say it was God's will after all." The rain fell around them; the wind whistled and shrieked. "Tell me again," he said.

"I do," she murmured. "I love you, Shawn Malone."

Both of them were shivering and totally drenched when Shawn suggested they go out to the boat and rescue Bear. "He's probably cowering under a berth, whimpering and whining," he said. "Besides that, he's probably starving."

"Where'd you tie up your dinghy?"

"Over there."

"Where?"

"Over—Hey! It's gone!"

They scrambled down the boulder and Theresa raced after him, backtracking to snatch her hat, then raced to keep up with his long strides and jumps over the strewn driftwood and logs. Ducking under low, overhanging arbutus branches, Shawn disappeared and she followed. They stood beneath the wet foliage.

"Can you beat that?" exclaimed Shawn, looking all around, waving his arms through the empty space. "Tied it right here, to this—Hey, look here! My rope!" He held up the frayed end.

"Looks like the storm knocked the boat around when the tide was up," she said, taking a closer look.

"I heard the wind last night, but didn't think it would come up this high," he said glumly. "Now what do we do? Can't swim for it."

"My uncle's got a dinghy out in the back shed. Help me look for the key and we can haul it out."

They found the key under the kitchen sink, hung over a nail set in the wood strip between the two cupboards. Shawn bounced the key on his hand. "Does that wind seem to be picking up to you?" he asked.

She listened. "Maybe."

"I don't like the sound of it." He opened the back door and stepped outside and the wind took his hair and blew it straight back. "You know, I'd feel a lot better if I had my boat moored properly. What do you say we haul out that dinghy of yours and pull up anchor and take *The Sailing Bear* down to the marina?"

Oh, the thrill of it, actually sailing such a magnificent ship, and in such weather. "Race you to the shed!" she called, darting past him, feeling like a child.

She pounded the steps hard in her boots, jumped the last two, and scaled three stumps before he caught up. Passing by he swooped her up and jogged with her in his arms. She bounced and clung and laughed. She was still laughing when he set her down in front of the shed. She laughed as he fished in his pocket for the key. But when he finally got the door open, it wasn't funny anymore. The shed was empty.

"You got any neighbors who can loan us a dinghy?"

"Only Charley—next door. But I saw him taking off yesterday."

"Come on, let's get out of this wind." He plopped an arm around her shoulders and they walked back to the cabin. Inside they tossed aside their rain-soaked jackets and wet socks and boots. Shawn stirred up the fire and threw on another log. "Your uncle got any duds around here that I might be able to wear?"

"In the bathroom. Bottom drawer. Might be snug, but they'll be dry." She went into the bedroom and pulled out a new sweatshirt and dry pants for herself. "What are you going to do about your dog?" she called through the closed door.

"I don't know! What am I going to do about my *boat*?"

"You finding anything to wear?"

"Yeah. Say, that Mama Mouse came back! Did I tell you?"

"I told *you*!" she hollered. "Remember?"

He came out wearing one of Ron's old shirts. The sleeves rode halfway up his forearms. The pants weren't much better, but at least they weren't Ron's. They were Uncle John's hunting pants. "What am I going to do about Bear?" he asked, pulling at the sleeves.

"Is he smart enough to open up his own Puppy Chow?" she quipped, trying to make him smile.

"Ah, I guess he'll be okay. He's been stranded before; this isn't the first time."

"And your boat?"

"That's not so easy. I don't know—"

"I know!" she exclaimed, trying to tease the smile out again. "We can pretend we're marooned. And we eat tomatoes out of tin cans, and read to each other in candlelight, and—"

"Just like in a very bad script," he interrupted. "Which would be fine, but I *am* worried about the boat. You say you've got a phone?"

"Mm-m."

"I'll call Ben George and see if he can't motor over and rescue me. At least let him know I can't make that meeting."

"Ben George? You know him?"

"Young Life days. We worked together."

"Well, the phone's over there."

"It's dead." Shawn dropped the receiver back into the cradle and glowered at it.

"Now what are you going to do?"

"I don't know. Swim, I guess."

"Don't you dare!" she declared, flying past him to throw herself against the front door. "If the rocks don't dash you to pieces, hypothermia will get you!"

"I can always go out the back door, you know."

He caught her as she flew past again and pinned her to the wall. "I love you," he said, dropping kisses over her face. "You didn't think I was serious, did you?"

"You silly," she said, feeling silly herself. "Let's eat."

"Let's fix breakfast first."

They sat down across from each other. "Let *me* say the blessing this time," said Shawn.

And so they prayed, but this time it was together—and over warm eggs.

CHAPTER 10

"Hey, not bad."

"Thank you," said Theresa, watching Shawn eat. He did it with vigor, as he tackled everything. He smiled and she smiled and outside the wind howled, a gray day turning black. But inside they were together, and it was wonderful. They were eating breakfast and Shawn had prayed and was now as "fanatical" as she was. The best part of all was that they were in love. It was hard to realize how good God really was.

"What shall we do," she asked melodramatically, "marooned as we are on the end of this God-forsaken island?"

"We're hardly marooned."

"That still leaves what are we going to do."

"I don't know. Got any ideas? Say, what's this on the toast?"

"Lemon cheese."

"What's lemon cheese?"

"You like it?"

"I *love* it."

"All Americans love it," she said, sitting up and taking proper pride in the exclusive Canadian jam. "Every time I come to Canada, I get four or five jars for everyone. Always thought it might make a good business; I could become a millionaire importing lemon cheese."

"Tastes kind of like lemon meringue pie, doesn't it?"

"You ought to try it on crumpets."

"Where was this stuff the other day?"

"Hiding. I found it when I was cleaning."

"May I put another piece of toast in?"

"Help yourself. Come up with any great plans for the day yet?"

"No. Thought you had some writing to do."

She grimaced. How could she write with *him* around? It was rather like stringing plastic beads while someone else was weaving golden beads onto a real necklace. The toaster popped and Shawn dropped two pieces onto his plate. "I can't write if you're around," she told him.

"Maybe we could brainstorm story ideas."

"What story ideas?"

"*Your* story ideas, honey. Remember you're supposed to be coming up with a book?"

"Actually, I'm supposed to be working on a short story."

"Forget the short story. You've got a book to write. We'll work on the story another day."

"You don't even know if I can write," she told him. Then she cocked her head. "What's that?"

"What?"

"There's a drip somewhere."

Shawn took his toast into the bedroom. "You've got a leak, it looks like. Rain's coming through the ceiling right beside the bed. And you're wrong. I *do* know you can write. I can just tell."

Theresa found a pot and stuck it under the drip. "Now it's *really* loud," she said.

Shawn steered her out. "I'm going to make you a cup of tea, then we're going to go into the living room and brainstorm. Before this wind is finished, I expect a hundred pages out of you."

"A hundred pages! How long do you think we'll be marooned?"

"We're hardly marooned. Come on, here we are. Set your feet up. That's it." He returned to the kitchen and began putting the dishes into the sink. "Somewhere in there," he said, talking to her over the divider and tapping his head and then pointing to her, "is the next Great American Novel. Where's the soap?"

"Under the sink."

He squirted too much into the running water and suds piled up. He poked the growing pile, then plunged both hands in and retrieved a plate, ran a washcloth over it, and set it into the drainer to his right.

For the next hour he drilled her about other events in her life and asked her what sorts of things she'd been learning. They drank their tea slowly, stopping once to fill the pot. He showed her how to take bits and pieces and construct a simple story idea. "I've got it! I've got my story!" she cried suddenly, as all the pieces fell into place. "I'll have this woman, and she'll—"

"Wait. Don't tell me. It'll ruin it—sap all your

141

energy and you'll lose it. Keep it locked up in your head until you get it down on paper. Just tell me your theme."

"Well, that God doesn't abandon us."

"Not clear enough. That doesn't mean anything."

"What do you mean, that doesn't mean anything?"

"All right, tell me what it means."

"It means that God doesn't promise to make it easy, but He promises to be with us." She groaned. "What an absolutely startling revelation. I'll sell a million copies."

"You could. It's not the theme. It's the telling. Nothing's new under the sun, as the late great Solomon said—once upon a time. But if you tell a good enough story, bring a new slant to the obvious— like how easy it is to forget such simple truths under hurt and confusion—if you make your characters real enough—"

"Do you realize what we're doing?" she interrupted.

"What's that?"

"We're talking about God just as if—"

"We're both fanatics," he finished for her. He tipped his cup, daring the tea to spill. "You know, last night after putting you to bed, I did a lot of reading in that musty old Bible you've got there. I'm almost embarrassed over what a state I'd gotten myself into. That'll be the power behind your story, you know. How easily forgotten—"

"It's kind of embarrassing how easily it's forgotten. It's really a childish sort of concept to have—the notion that God is somehow like a fairy godmother with a magic wand."

"Well!" he said, setting aside his cup and getting

up. "You want another cup? Or are you all drunk up?"

"No, thanks. Do you mind if I start writing?"

"What? And leave me here with nothing to do?"

"There are books. Louis L'Amour and everything. And you must have writing of your own to do."

"You know," he said, "that's what I love about you. No sense of obligation toward anyone."

"I'll dedicate the book to you."

He chuckled and plucked a book off the shelf, and once again she marveled at the turn in her life. "Give me a pile of that paper," he said, turning around with a smile. "And a pen if you've got one. Hey, don't you have a blue one?"

"What's the matter with black?"

"I can't write with black. Black drives me crazy."

"You are crazy. Here."

"It's still dead.

"What is?"

"The phone."

Once in a while she heard him get up and move around. Once he went outside for a bit and the wind tore in. Now and then he brought her a cup of tea, and several times he emptied the rainpot in the bedroom. Only after a long time was she aware that she needed to stretch. It was three o'clock.

Shawn had fallen asleep on the chesterfield. He looked like a little boy instead of a strapping six foot six man. His legs hung over the chesterfield at the knee. Papers were scattered across the floor; more sat on his chest, as if he had fallen asleep reading them. She knelt beside him and collected the papers off his chest.

Even in sleep he was handsome, she thought. Thick

lashes rested against his cheeks. His forehead was square, his jaw not so square in sleep. She put a hand to his chest to feel the rise and fall as he breathed. A tenderness came to her, and gratitude to God almost overpowering in its intensity. Full of love she bent over him. "I love you," she whispered.

He blinked, then opened his eyes, bringing one arm up to rest over his forehead. "Are the fairy tales backwards in Canada?"

"Pardon?"

"Are the fairy tales backwards in Canada?" He touched her cheek and rubbed his thumb over her jawline. "In the States it's the handsome prince who awakens the beautiful princess. But here the beautiful princess—"

"You are so silly." She gazed down into his beautiful marble-brown eyes. "Now I know what people mean when they say they can drown in someone's eyes." She rubbed her own thumb over *his* jawline. He leaned into her touch and kissed her thumb. She liked the way his lips moved when he was about to smile.

He kissed her thumb again. "What about drowning in people's eyes?" he asked lazily.

"I could drown in your eyes, that's all."

"Funny, I was just thinking the same thing about yours. Did you know you have gray stars in the middle of your blue eyes?"

"Lopsided stars."

"They're beautiful lopsided stars."

"You want to know something?" she said. "I didn't think I could ever fall in love with someone with brown eyes. I've always liked blue for some reason." She kissed him. "Didn't know what I was missing."

He lay quietly. She knelt quietly. Suddenly he stirred.

"The wind."

"What about it?"

"It's getting worse." He sat and put his hands under her arms and pulled her up beside him. She let him kiss her face, tiny kisses all over her skin. "I'm going to have to leave this little love nest," he whispered, "and get going."

"But we don't have a dinghy. We're marooned, remember?" She turned her cheek for more little pecks, lost in the swirling sensations of his touch. He kissed her neck and murmured something she couldn't hear and brought her face straight. She thought she might never be the same when he tilted her forehead to meet his.

"There's the back road," he whispered.

She groaned. "I was hoping you'd forget that route."

He chuckled. "No such luck. Got a memory like a horse."

"You really think you have to go?"

"I've got to get my boat in. It's worrying me. And Bear must be a wreck by now."

"But walking down a back road seems to be going the wrong way."

"Ah! But at the end of the road is help. At the end of the road is someone with an outboard who can buzz me over here."

"And then you'll stay."

"Persistent little thing, aren't you?"

"Please?" She grabbed tight around his neck so he couldn't get away.

"Hey, I can't stay here all night again."

"Why not?"

"For one thing, I have to get my boat down to the marina."

"Come back for a game of Scrabble."

"Scrabble? Hey, am I squishing you?"

"No. Stay right where you are. Every cabin has a Scrabble game. Even I know that."

"I can't come back. I can't spend another night here."

"Why not?"

"What'll I tell Mr. McCullough? You may not be worried about *your* reputation, but—"

She laughed. "So then tell me what your plans are. Will I see you again?"

"Of course you'll see me!"

"You'll come back—eventually?"

He kissed her. "Of course I'll come back. I promise."

"When?"

"I don't know."

"You're so secretive. How come?"

He laughed out loud. "Secretive? Me? I'm an open book."

"Then tell me when I'll see you again, and what you're going to be doing when you're not seeing me."

"My, my. Not only are you persistent, but you're a nosy little thing, too."

"Me and Mr. McCullough."

"Are you feeling a little insecure?" he asked suddenly, his eyes growing serious and concerned. She nodded, afraid to let him know how frightened she was actually getting. She couldn't shake the fear that she might never see him again.

"You are, aren't you?" he said.

"I think I am."

"Well, I *can't* let you know when I'll be back. My days don't work that way. I'm doing research. And I never know how long it will take me because I don't know what I'll find."

"What are you researching?"

"My next book."

"I assumed that! *What* are you researching?"

"Didn't I tell you?"

"You did not."

"Thetis Island."

"You're kidding! Really and truly?"

"Really and truly. I came across an old Indian legend and I think Thetis is the point of origin. Anyway, I'm making up a story about it."

A sudden boom rattled the cabin. Shawn was up in a flash. "What was that?"

"Is your boat still there?"

"It's there. But it's nasty out. Well, that settles it. I'm walking. I should have done it two hours ago."

He started into his jacket. "Does your uncle have a hat I can borrow?"

"Cupboard in the bedroom. You want something to take with you—an apple or something?"

"Sounds good. What time is it, anyway?" he called, his voice muffled through the wall.

"Three-thirty!" She pulled on her own jacket, a heavy rubber raincoat.

"What do you think you're doing?" he demanded when he saw her.

"I'm going to go with you."

"Oh, no, you're not. You're going to stay right here where it's warm and dry and safe."

"Where a tree can fall on my head, you mean. Darn

147

this zipper. It *never* wants to zip up. Here, will you help me?"

"I will not. Take that off. You're not going anywhere."

"I'm not staying here all by myself."

"Theresa, it's blowing up into a regular gale out there. Any minute now we're going to get thunder and lightning. How did it get so bad? I've got to hurry. Where's that apple?"

"I'm going with you."

"Theresa, don't be foolish. How would I get you back here?"

"*You're* coming back, aren't you?"

"Only to get my boat. Then I have to get it into the marina—where it can be out of the worst of it. That's the whole idea, Theresa."

"You can drop me off then."

"No."

"Shawn, I'm scared. I don't want to be left out here all by myself."

His jaw tightened. "All right, then. I haven't time to stand around here arguing. But hurry up, we're wasting time."

"My zipper?"

He zipped it up, jerking it past the tight spot. "You got your boots?"

The wind hit them hard when they stepped out, and the rain drove like needles into Theresa's face. She yanked her toque down around her ears, grateful for the warm wool. "Whew! You think your boat will be all right until we get back?"

"Better be."

He walked close, arm around her back, and neither of them spoke. The wind was too loud to outshout, and they needed their energy to keep moving. When they passed two trees that had apparently blown down, the thought occurred to Theresa that one might very well come down on her head.

Dear Lord, she prayed. *Do keep those trees standing until we get past.* Then she remembered and amended her prayer. *Lord, take away this fright. Help me to know You're with me.*

It took nearly an hour to reach Mr. McCullough's store, but no trees fell across their way, and the jangle of the bells as they closed the door was a welcome sound after the fury outside. Theresa was too exhausted even to say hello, but stumbled past the astounded Mr. McCullough to the nearest table, and sank into the chair. Shawn dropped into the chair across from her and she felt his feet slide next to hers.

"Heavens!" exclaimed the old proprietor in alarm, bustling around the cash register and hurrying over. "Don't tell me you've been out in this! Theresa, what in the blazes—You look as white as a shortbread cookie!"

"I'm freezing!" she choked, chin chattering. "My hands. . . . "

"Have you got a warm towel, or something that she can put them in?" Shawn asked, unzipping his soaked jacket, revealing the shirt that was too small.

"Of course. Let me get one. I'll be right back."

"You okay, honey?" he asked, peering into her face.

She tried a weak grin. After all, she'd been out there through her own choice, against Shawn's wishes. "Sure. Are you?"

"I'm okay. The thought of going out again isn't a cheery one, though. Mr. McCullough, have you got an outboard I can borrow?"

"Sure, but—"

"I've got my boat anchored out by Theresa's place. Need to get it in!"

"Well, certainly. Yes. You need to do it immediately. This wind. Let me get my coat. I'll go with you. Theresa—"

"No, I can handle it. No sense the two of us getting wet. You got anything Theresa can change into?"

"I thought I was going to go back with you!" She flung the warm towel aside. "Shawn," she cried, when she saw his face. "You promised—"

"Theresa, no."

"*Shawn*."

"You can't. And that's that."

"But, Shawn!"

"No!"

She wiped a cold hand across her face. Mr. McCullough tried to get her to take the warm towel. "Honey, it's too windy out there," said Shawn, taking the towel and wrapping her hands once again, then holding her hands firmly with his own. "I didn't know it would get so bad. I can't let you go out there. Look at the water. Look at it, honey."

Water slammed against the tidewall, sending spray over the window. "But what about you?"

"I'll be okay."

"You can't go all by yourself. You can't. Don't! Please don't go!" The water was crashing furiously over the rocks. The tied-up boats slammed against the docks.

"Please," she cried. Then, to herself, *God, please don't let him go*.

"I have to go get my boat. I have to go get Bear," Shawn kept saying, but she clung to his arm, and cried and pleaded, aware that she was acting like a child, but helpless to stop herself. Shawn was going to take an outboard into that storm, and she'd be left behind to pick up the pieces, just as she'd had to do with her mother and father.

Mr. McCullough pulled her loose.

"You go on now," he said to Shawn. "I'll take care of her. The key's in the ignition. It's *Swell*. Dock A-3."

"Shawn, Shawn, you'll drown and I'll never see you again," she cried, running after him as the awful truth came out. How could she trust God to keep him safe? God would just let him disappear and she would never see him again. The awful truth bounced off the walls. "Shawn! Please don't go!"

She tasted the salt of her tears, and then the fresh rain on Shawn's jacket. She bit her hand to bring pain, to check her panic, but it was all out of control and she could only sob, "Don't go, don't go, please don't go."

"Shh," he whispered, kissing her forehead and taking her in his arms. "Shh. Remember what we were talking about? The theme to your new story—"

"No," she cried. "He won't. It's going to be just like before. He's useless when it comes to things that really matter. He'll let you drown, I'll never see you again."

"I'll be okay. I'll wear a life preserver. I promise. And remember, God *is* with us."

"A lot of good that will do."

"Stop it." He gripped her upper arms with his hands, planting her to the floor. She couldn't move.

"Stop it," he said again sternly. "I *have* to go. I can't let my boat be dashed to pieces, but it's not that suicidal out there. I just don't want *you* out in it."

151

"Please don't go," she pleaded, begging him with her eyes, imploring him. She would do anything to keep him from leaving. The wonderful jigsaw puzzle that came together in her head this morning was gone, and all that was left was waves and crashing trees and the lightning now jumping out of the sky.

"Theresa, what about all we talked about this morning?" he demanded, shaking her, gripping her arms until they hurt. "Remember? All that business about God not promising to keep us safe, but promising to be with us? Remember that? Isn't that what we talked about? Isn't that the theme of your new story? That He never leaves us, nor forsakes us?"

"It's all just words and ideas. What if a big wave comes, or what if you slip when you're getting on board, or what if—"

"Hush." He put a hand over her mouth. "If I drown, *if* I drown, God will still be with you. *If* I drown, God will be with me. But I won't drown. All the tea in China can't keep me from coming back to you."

"Come, come, lass," Mr. McCullough said quietly. "You need to be letting him go. The sooner he's off, the sooner he's back."

Shawn's face was gray. "Honey, I won't go until you're okay. Are you okay?"

She started to cry again, weakly this time, her panic spent, and shame over her outburst catching up with her. "I'm sorry. I don't know what got into me— went a little crazy. You've got to go get your boat. It'll be ruined if it breaks loose. I'm sorry."

He smiled wanly. "Maybe you went just a *little* crazy," he teased. "You all right now?"

"I'm all right. The sooner you go, the sooner you get back."

"One for the road, eh?"

She kissed him and held him as if the world might be gone if she let go.

"See?" he said. "You got me saying it now."

"What's that?"

"Saying *eh*." He pulled away. "I'll be back."

"Grab my Mackintosh on your way out, Mr. Malone. Should help keep the spray off you."

"It's Shawn. And thanks, Mr. McCullough. Take care of her, will you?"

"That I will—a good drubbing and a pot of tea." The bells jingled and Mr. McCullough led her into his living quarters in the back.

"I'm sorry, Mr. McCullough," she said, trailing forlornly after him. "I don't know why I got so crazy."

"Now, now, don't be so hard on yourself. It's understandable, what you been through. Now, here's the bath." He fussed around, got out clean towels, handed her a warm robe. "It'll be a little big, but you can wrap it tight and tie a knot. You got everything you need now, lassie?"

"I think so," she said, looking around, glad of some time to herself. She needed to sort herself out.

"Well, you just take your time. Don't come out until you're good and hot."

"All right, Mr. McCullough. But if Shawn comes back, you'll call me?"

"If you're in here that long, you'll be a dried-up prune, you will."

She'd never been in Mr. McCullough's living quarters before. They were nice. The bathroom was old-fashioned, with a claw-foot tub and a toilet with the water tank high on the wall. Cracked and sparkled linoleum poked out from under four different floor rugs.

She slipped out of her clothes and lay them in a sopping pile near the door while the bathwater ran. A puddle grew and spread and she threw a towel down to catch it. Poor Shawn. He was out there in the rain, fighting the wind. Bear would probably knock him into the water.

No, she was not going to think about Shawn until he got back, and she would not think about what a fool she'd made of herself, either. What had gotten into her, anyway?

But she knew.

No, don't think about it, she told herself.

But she couldn't *not* think. She'd made a fool out of herself, and the worst of it was that she had dragged God into it all again. She *had* to think about it. She had to figure it out.

The tub water was hot and she inched in slowly, exhaling as she slithered into the heat. The clean towels were draped over the back of the tub and she leaned her head against them. *God, are You really with us all the time?* she asked. *Even when the worst happens?*

It was quiet. She couldn't hear the wind in here. Her thoughts grew quiet, too, and she grew sleepy from the heat and the aftermath of her outburst.

"I count your tears and put them in a bottle." It was the still, small voice of God and it came from the empty space of the room, or from way deep inside her. She saw the agates, the Apache tears, in the milk bottle, and her own tears in Gods's bottle somewhere.

154

And she remembered God's promise for a future of good, not evil. And peace found its way into her heart.

"Forgive me for forgetting so easily, Lord," she whispered, as the peace that passeth all understanding worked its way back in.

What seemed like hours later she toweled herself dry. *I'm crying again*, she realized. But it didn't matter. They were different tears and God collected such tears. Tears of pain and tears of understanding, He collected them all.

"Thank you, Lord," she whispered, then tied the knot on Mr. McCullough's robe.

Mr. McCullough took her bundle of clothes and disappeared through a back door. "I didn't know you had a door into the laundromat, Mr. McCullough," she called.

He tossed the pile into a dryer. "There's lots of things you don't know, lass. Now, you sit right there and I'll get you something hot. You look a bit better. That bath fixed you up good, didn't it? I was worried about you."

"I'm sorry. I guess I got a little hysterical."

"A little?"

"All right, a lot. When do you think he'll be back?"

"Who? That Shawn Malone? It's only been an hour, eh? Give him another one. Here, I fixed you chowder and fries."

He settled into the chair across from her, hands over his stomach, and waited while she said grace. Outside the wind howled.

"Amen. You up to telling me what's going on between you and that American, lass?"

"I'm sorry I made such a scene."

"That not what I'm talking about. And that's fine. You did just fine. What I want to know is—when did you fall in love with that man?"

She looked up sharply, a french fry poised in midair. "Is it that obvious?" She realized the stupidity of the question as soon as she said it.

"Now that's a silly question. I've never seen you hysterical over *Ron* before! And I've seen a lot o' you and Ron, lass."

It was surprising how a hot bath, time to think, a good long cry, and an inquisitive friend made her feel like her old self again. "I think falling in love must be like falling out of bed when you're asleep," she said. "You just wake up on the floor."

"So you love him."

"I love him."

"When did you figure it out?"

"Last night. No, this morning. Oh, I don't know! Maybe I fell in love with him when I saw my pink blouse hanging way up there on the mast of *The Sailing Bear!*"

"Does he treat you good?"

"I've never been treated better."

"What about Ron?"

"I didn't mean to speak against Ron, Mr. McCullough."

"I know you didn't. It's just that I'm mighty fond of Ron."

"I'm fond of Ron, too. It really bothers me—" Why was she telling him all this. "It'll just have to be different from now on. Too much water under the bridge," she added, seeing Mr. McCullough's face. "Mr. McCullough, I've fallen in love with Shawn.

And I think he's better for me. He's a writer, did you know? We have the same interests, the same direction. Ron and I. . . . Where are your customers, Mr. McCullough? Where is the post office lady?"

"You think anybody sane would be out in this weather?"

She laughed, then thought of Shawn with a painful twinge. "No, I guess not."

"What are you going to do about Ron?" he asked.

"What do you mean by that?"

"His wanting to marry you."

"He jilted me."

Mr. McCullough leaned forward. "Lass, I may not know what all went on between you two, but I do know this. It's never too late. You can always put up a new bridge when the old one is washed out, eh?"

"It *is* too late. I love Shawn."

"What do you *know* about him?" Mr. McCullough nearly snapped at her, and she was taken aback. He'd never sounded so harsh before. Then he seemed to remember himself and leaned back. "Ron's wanting to take that job at Capernwray."

"Then why doesn't he?"

"Because they've offered it to Shawn Malone, that's why. The job that Ron had his heart set on— they gave it to your Shawn Malone. Big, fancy Shawn Malone from the States."

The whole world went cold. "No."

"He's an American, lass. Unscrupulous. Tyrannical. Dictatorial—"

"But when? How? He didn't say anything about— Are you *sure*, Mr. McCullough?"

"Ron came by this morning to tell me."

She pushed away the fries and soup. "I can hardly believe it."

Mr. McCullough rose tight-lipped and began to clear the dishes.

"Wait a minute," she called after him. "That's not possible, Mr. McCullough. Ron is a psychiatrist. Shawn is a writer. They're two different kinds of people and they don't apply for the same kind of job. There's some mistake."

He set a fresh cup of tea in front of her. "Didn't Ron tell you what that job was all about?"

"I guess I didn't let him," she whispered, feeling sick and weary and confused all of a sudden. *What was it that he had said about that job?*

"It seems they're looking to set up some sort of lay ministry, a community counseling center or something. I'm not too good at the lingo and all that, eh, but they told Ron they're not particularly interested in hiring someone with the degree. The intention, I guess, is to bring about a system where people help each other."

"That still doesn't make any sense. Shawn's a writer. He's not interested in counseling anybody. He's smack dab in the middle of researching his next book."

"And he's going to write it while he helps the guy over there set the program up."

"Ben George?"

"That's the one."

The world grew colder and the wind came to her ears. Salt spray dashed against the window. "He had an appointment with Ben George this afternoon," she said, watching the spray stream down the window.

"See? What did I tell you?"

"Ben George and Shawn were friends in Seattle; worked together in Young Life," she said flatly.

"That's what Mr. George told Ron. Said he knew he could work well with Shawn, that Shawn—"

"Stop! I don't want to hear anymore."

Outside the storm raged. Inside a new one began to rumble. How could Shawn have done that? How could he have taken Ron's job? How could he talk about writing, and loving her, and never mention something so important as working at Capernwray? Why, they had even talked about Capernwray. How could he not have known that Ron wanted the job? Research, indeed.

The cold inside turned to ice and she thought she'd be sick. *That's* what that meeting today was supposed to be all about. Shawn had been deliberately evasive, as persistent as she had been. He *must* have known about Ron. Of all the low-down, sly things to do. And here she was thinking. . . . What *had* she been thinking? What *was* she thinking?

"Mr. McCullough?"

"Yes, lass?"

"I don't think I want to be here when he comes back."

"What are you going to do, lass?"

"I don't know. Go home, I guess. Will you drive me out? Or can't you leave the store?"

"No, no, that's fine. No one'll be showing up anyway, 'cepting your Shawn."

"I just need time to think, you know?"

"Sure you do. Your clothes are dry. Soon as you change I'll take you home. Can you use a bag of all-sorts?"

"Yes, Mr. McCullough, that would be real nice."

CHAPTER 11

THERESA SAT AT THE typewriter, poking at the keys, drinking coffee into the night.

In the morning she read what she'd written. She liked it. What's more, it was good. Since the Red Rose tea was all gone from the Peak Frean's tin, she made some instant coffee and fixed a small omelet from what was left of Shawn's groceries.

Shawn.

As much as she tried not to think of him, she did. A lot. She thought about what they had said, too. Imaginary scenes played and replayed in her mind since she left him with no explanation. None of them were any good. In some, she'd grow angry with Shawn for not coming after her, the way all the Harlequin heroes did. Sometimes the melodrama went to the tune of his seeking her out on bended knee, begging forgiveness for having deceived her. At other times the drama switched, and it was she who begged. How foolish of her to have walked off like that!

Leaving without a word, not even waiting for an explanation. But then, what sort of explanation could he have offered to acquit himself? None. And the horrid little play switched back.

She spent much of the time focusing on her book. The main character, Sally, was a lot like Theresa, only more beautiful, more daring—more everything. She was everything Theresa longed to be. And the hero, of course, was everything heroes were supposed to be. Tender and passionate, seeking out damsels in distress.

For a full week Theresa wrote. Her days fell into a routine—up at sunrise, shower, breakfast, then Bible reading out on the patio. In going through the Gospels, Theresa found that Jesus never turned His back on anyone. So much for abandonment on God's part.

After Bible reading came cleaning—sweeping sand out of the house, pulling back the curtains. One day she even took down the yellow priscillas and ironed them. The last thing she did before sitting down to the typewriter was to take some agates out of the *Chehalis Dairy* bottle and spread them on the window sill. Apache tears, Shawn had called them. As she put them back in, she tried to think of God collecting her tears, taking away the pain and feelings of abandonment. It was better than carrying it around with her.

Eventually Shawn's groceries ran out and she had to go back to the marina. Plot and dialogue and her heroine's adventures filled her thoughts as she made her way over the familiar beach, and she stopped only once to peer into a tide pool. When she got to McCullough's store, she hesitated before swinging the door open.

"I didn't hear you come in, lass."

"You ought to do something about those bells, Mr. McCullough. They drive me nuts! I *tried* not to make them jingle."

His eyebrows went up. The old lady with the white hair sat back in the corner sorting the mail. Everything was the same.

"The last I saw him," said Mr. McCullough, "was right after I got back from taking you home, eh? He ain't been in since then."

"Did I ask about him, Mr. McCullough?"

"No, but you were wanting to know, eh? How are you doing, anyway? Haven't seen you for a week."

He followed her as she went up and down the grocery shelves, picking out what she needed. His prices were terrible. She really should take the ferry over to Chemainus and stock up.

"I'm doing fine. Say, I've started a book."

"So you're still writing, are you? What's it about?"

"Can't tell you. Shawn said—"

Mr. McCullough's smile vanished. Theresa didn't know quite how to continue, so she went around the corner to a new shelf. "He said it would take all my energy away if I let it out anywhere except on paper."

"Oh. Well, that's a good idea. *Sounds* like a good idea, anyway." His voice trailed off as he returned to the checkout stand. She heard the clump, clump of his shoes on the planking.

"What did you tell him when he came back?" she asked. Then she held her breath and stared at Nabob, the fat little Arabian boy, the logo of Nabob's Lemon Cheese selling for $3.25 for eight ounces. How many hours had she wondered, and worried, about the answer to that question?

"I didn't tell him anything."

"Will you tell me what happened? You must have said something."

"There ain't much to tell. He asked where you were. I said you'd wanted to go home. He looked kind of surprised. Then he just said thanks for taking care of you, and the next day he was gone."

"Did you tell him why I left?"

"No."

"Has Ron been in?"

"No."

Mr. McCullough plucked little Nabob up in his hand and strode to the counter. "It's a nice day. Why don't you borrow that fishing rod of mine again and go out and get yourself some nice fish for supper—like you did the time before? Would taste mighty good with crumpets and lemon cheese."

"I need to get back and write. And besides, you're too expensive to be buying crumpets and lemon cheese from."

"My treat," he said seriously. He stood at the register, jam on the counter, his hand over the lid, waiting.

Suddenly she wanted to cry. "I don't want to go fishing, Mr. McCullough," she said.

"You can't just hole yourself up in that cabin out there, banging your hurt out on a typewriter. You've got to go out and punch something. Get some exercise. Go find Ron."

She ignored that last suggestion and finished her shopping. Other customers drifted in and out and she listened to the casual banter of voices, the bang of the bells, the cash drawer sliding open and shut as Mr. McCullough made change. When it was finally quiet she lined up her purchases along the counter next to the lemon cheese and said, "Maybe I *will* go for a walk. I'll go see if that starfish has grown his leg back yet."

"What starfish?"

"The kids out at Capernwray cut off a starfish's leg—an experiment or something—they said it would grow back. I've been wondering if it's true. May I leave my stuff here and pick it up on my way home?"

"Sure. I'll put your bag in the fridge."

The walk to the public wharf and ferry slip was not as far as the walk out to the cabin, and she reached it in minutes. Warmth oozed out of the wooden planks of the public wharf, and Theresa took off her sandals, stepping carefully to avoid getting splinters in her feet, and enjoying the heat. At the end of the wharf a small fiberglass dingy bobbed in the water, squeaking against the rubber tires tied to the edge.

Theresa loved this part of the island, not only because of the Mission, but because the scenery never failed to move her by its beauty. She could see the small islands—Kuper and Airport Strip and Burnt Island and the others she didn't know the names of. Airport Strip was called that because some rich man who lived there owned a plane and had swathed out the forest, putting in a runway that cut the small island in half. Only by boating past the north and south ends could you even see the scar.

Burnt Island was Burnt Island because a long time ago it had burned down to bare rock. It was only about a city block big, and was full of sharp, deep crevices and huge boulders, and was rich in sea life. Grasses and stumps grew now, and wild flowers.

To the west was Vancouver Island, with smoke

coming out of the Chemainus, Nanaimo, and Duncan sawmills. It was beautiful country. It was soothing just to be here.

It was always inky black below the pier. What she really liked to do was to take a boat under there; it was like exploring a cavern. She could see the pilings, inky with creosote, splotched with barnacles and mussels, seaweed lacing them together like cobwebs in an attic. The starfish hugged the pilings like purple quilted pillows sewn to a post.

It took fifteen minutes, lying on her stomach at the end of the wharf, to find it. It had moved, but there was no mistaking the growing stub. "So they really do grow new legs," she muttered, head hanging down, hair blowing in the breeze.

The shadows in the water fascinated her, rippling and growing light and dark. Her own shadow resembled kelp . . .

"Hi."

Theresa rolled her head sideways and saw Ron standing in the sun. "What are you doing?" he asked.

She was surprised to see him. She'd assumed he'd gone home, having lost the job. But she was glad to see him. He looked good, handsome as ever, his eyes clear and confident.

"Come see," she responded, and when he spread out beside her it was almost like old times. "See that starfish down there?" she asked. "It's growing a new leg. Did you know they did that?"

"Seems like I read it somewhere. Who cut it off?"

"The kids of Capernwray."

"Fredrick and Charles?"

"Mm-m."

"How are the mice?"

165

"They're doing fine. The mother came back."

The ferry tooted and they looked up to watch it come in. Six cars revved their motors, the gate clanked down, the foot passengers walked off, and then the cars followed, clanking and banging as they drove over the iron ramps. Then it all happened in reverse. Motors in the line-up revved, foot passengers walked on board, the cars followed, clanking and banging. The iron ramps were raised and locked and the water boiled as the ferry backed out and turned.

"I'm sorry, Theresa," said Ron. "I'm sorry about this whole mess."

"Which mess do you mean?" She was still hanging upside-down, peering into the gloom under the dock.

"The mess with that boyfriend of yours."

"It's certainly not your fault."

"It is."

His voice was funny and she twisted her head to look at him. A funny feeling stirred in the pit of her stomach and she dropped her head again to lose herself under the dock. "Maybe you'd better explain yourself."

"It wasn't intentional."

"What wasn't intentional, Ron?" It irritated her the way it took him so long to explain anything, as though he had to consider each word a hundred times before he said it.

"It surprised me, you know. Your falling for that guy so fast."

She bit her tongue and waited. He'd get to it sooner or later.

"I must say, it took me back a bit, and I don't think I was especially nice about it."

"You weren't."

"After I left you that day," he went on, "I went back to Capernwray to see if I could spend the night. That was when Ben told me he wanted to talk to Shawn about the job I had interviewed for—the job that was basically all sewed up, remember? Remember he said the job was pretty much mine, that there was only the paperwork to be done? That he had another interview but I looked 'A-okay?'"

The funny feeling in her stomach turned to nausea. She concentrated on the starfish.

"Why don't you look at me? You're not making this very easy, you know."

She glanced up briefly. "If I don't stare at this stupid starfish, I'll probably scream or something."

"Scream? At me?"

"You. Me. What difference does it make?"

"I was down at the marina. Mr. McCullough told me that he told you that I told him that Shawn was taking that job. Diagram *that* sentence."

"He told me they *gave* Shawn your job."

"Well, that isn't exactly true."

"Not exactly true!" She nearly choked. "What do you mean, not exactly true?" She skinned her knee scrambling to her feet, and the blood rushing out of her head left her dizzy. She sat back down. "Start at the beginning."

"What's the beginning?" he sighed.

"Did they or did they not offer Shawn your job?"

"Ben told me that night he wanted to interview Shawn. He was going to do it the next day, then let me know one way or another."

"Did he or did he not, Ron?"

"The day of the interview was the day we got that storm."

167

"And Shawn didn't show up—because he was out at the cabin." New puzzle pieces were falling into place and Theresa didn't like the picture that was forming. "Shawn had no idea what that meeting was all about, did he?"

"No."

A boat went by. She waited for the wake to roll in. It sloshed against the pilings; then there came the quiet lap, lap again. Theresa focused on a bent arbutus in the cliff just to the right of the wharf.

"I couldn't believe it when Ben told me he wanted to talk to Shawn," she heard Ron saying. "It was kind of a double whammy, you know. First he walks off with my girl—"

"I'm not your girl."

"—and then he walks off with my job. And when I saw Mr. McCullough the next morning, it all sort of spilled out, I guess."

"But Shawn didn't want your job. He didn't even know there *was* a job!"

"Well, I thought he did. At first. All right, I *assumed* he did. Thought he'd requested the interview, that he'd applied for it. How was I to know any different? I didn't find out till later that Ben was just exploring the possibilities. I was just—"

"Never mind," she interrupted again. "How come you didn't clear it up once you found out different?"

"That's nasty, Theresa."

"Well, why didn't you? Why didn't you come tell me? Why didn't you—"

"I didn't find out until last night."

"What happened last night?" she demanded.

"I talked with Ben George. He offered me the job, for sure. Seems Shawn wasn't interested. Ben couldn't get hold of him, or something."

She held her head between her hands and squeezed against her temples. New pain zigzagged behind her eyes. Shawn hadn't known about any job. And if he had, of course he wouldn't have wanted a job at Capernwray anyway. How could she have even *thought* he would? How could any of them have thought that he would?

Ron, because he was feeling jealous, and angry, and a little up-ended. Mr. McCullough, because he had an irrational distrust of Americans. And she? Why had she jumped to such a ridiculous conclusion?

An ache worse than anything she had known grew inside. Hot, smarting tears stung behind her eyelids and she blinked rapidly. How could she have been so foolish? So childish? He would never forgive her. And running off the way she had with no explanation? Such a stupid and cruel thing to do. The irony of it all came to her in a black cloud of despair. All through life she'd been blaming God for abandoning her and letting awful things happen, when in reality—at least this time around—it was *she* who had done the abandoning.

"Look, I'm sorry," said Ron.

"It's hardly your fault," she mumbled, fighting hard to stay in control. "It's my own making. If I hadn't run off. . . ."

"Why did you run off?" he asked kindly. "Without waiting to ask him what the story was?"

"I thought it was kind of a sneaky thing to do, taking your job away." She hugged her knees with her elbows, still pushing the heels of her hands against her temples.

"I didn't know you cared."

She could feel his eyes on her. "Of course I care,"

169

she said, not holding back the tears anymore. "You've worked hard all these years, and I know how you love Thetis. And you wanted that job. I may not want to marry you anymore, Ron, but that doesn't mean I haven't stopped wanting what would make you happy. Working here at Thetis would be perfect for you." She wiped her eyes. "Oh, it's a fine state we're all in, isn't it?"

He got up and wandered along the edge of the pier, stopping now and then to look back at her. "Do you remember that little conversation we had a few weeks ago?" he asked after a time. "Or rather, *I* had with you, about how we only loved each other out of need and all that?"

"I remember."

He grimaced. "I was sort of hoping you wouldn't." He shoved his hands into his pockets and teetered on the edge of the dock, balancing himself on the balls of his feet. It was a game they used to play, to see who went over first. She was too miserable now to pay much attention.

"Come here," he said. "I want to take another look at that starfish. Something just occurred to me." He sprawled onto the pier. "Come here!"

"What about it?" she said, lowering herself next to him.

"Starfish have eyes on the ends of their feet," he said. "Well, sort-of eyes, anyway—little sensory organs that come close to being eyes. Getting one of their legs severed puts their system into trauma. Just as when we go through a bit of trauma at upsets in our lives."

Theresa settled herself into the long discourse. He usually ended up somewhere, if you waited long enough.

"It just occurred to me that if starfish grow new appendages, then they have to grow new eyes. They can regain their perspective—once they're whole again, that is. Once the trauma subsides, they have new eyes to deal with life. New ways of looking at things. You know what I mean."

It all sounded a little psychological to her. It sounded like Ron talking.

"What I keep thinking about the starfish," she said, propping her chin on her hands, "is that if they can grow new legs, we can grow new hearts. You know, all the cracks and broken pieces and everything. I keep hoping—"

"I'm sorry, Theresa, I really am. I didn't mean to break your heart."

"It happened. No use in apologizing for it."

Ron scooted back and rolled over so that he lay with his face to the sky. "There's no chance for us, is there?"

All she could think of was Shawn, and what she had done. Ron waited. "No," she said.

"Not even with this Shawn fellow gone?"

"No, I don't think so."

He sighed again, an explosion of weariness and surrender. "I need you, Theresa. That's what I was trying to say. And I guess that's why I'm struggling to hang onto this eye analogy. We can't love each other out of need. We just can't. But that's how I love you." He rolled over, propped his chin in his hands, and looked at her. "Oh, what are we going to do with ourselves?"

"I guess the same thing as that old starfish under there."

"Grow new legs, or eyes, as the case may be?"

She nodded.

"Easier said than done."

She nodded again. Easier said than done, that was the truth. But she would learn how to do it. One thing she had learned through all this was that God was around, hanging in there with her.

Still Ron's eyes held her. "That's not fair," she said suddenly.

"What isn't?"

"Looking at me that way. Trying to make me feel guilty."

"You're right." He stood and held out a hand. "Come on, I'll walk you back. Then maybe we'd better say goodbye—for a while. But let's take the road. I don't feel like battling the rocks."

As they neared the marina Theresa said, "I have to stop off and get my groceries. Mr. McCullough's holding them for me. You want to come in?"

"No. Maybe I'll just say goodbye here."

She kissed his cheek quickly. "Come have tea sometime, will you? One of these days? You took the job, didn't you?"

"Yes, I took it." His smile was weak. "Goodbye now, eh?"

"You'll come for tea?"

"I don't think so."

"But Ron, can't we find some way to be friends?"

"Sure we can. But it'll take time. Those starfish don't grow new feet overnight."

"So it's goodbye? Right here in front of McCullough's Marina? Just like that?"

"Just like that. But it'll get better. Goodbye, Theresa."

She watched him take the road again, going back the way they'd come.

It seemed symbolic to her. His back grew smaller and smaller, then a bend in the road took him completely from sight.

"Goodbye, Ron," she whispered.

CHAPTER 12

"IF HE LOVES YOU, he'll come back."

"No, Mr. McCullough, I don't think so." Theresa stood at the counter of the marina, her bag of groceries resting on the counter. The proprietor stood beside his register looking sad and thoughtful.

"I say," he said, "I'm sorry for the part I played in it."

"I shouldn't have believed you, you know. I should have remembered how much you hate Americans."

He looked miserable and then she felt sorry for him. "Oh, don't take it so personally. It was my fault. But really, Mr. McCullough, you've got to get over that, you know."

He nodded. "Good habit to break, I'm guessing."

"Ah, but you can do it."

"I am sorry, Theresa Parker. If there's anything I can do. . . . "

"No. It was all my doing, I'm afraid. I behaved poorly." She picked up the bag.

"You mark my words now. If he loves you, he'll come back."

"Oh, Mr. McCullough," she exclaimed, feeling despair at the futility of his words. "Why would he do that? For one thing, I went off and left him with no explanation—after nearly throwing myself at him two hours earlier, I might add. He's going to think I'm crazy. And for another thing, if he ever finds out *why* I left—and I don't know how he'd ever find out—why, he'd never forgive me! And why should he?"

"Don't be so sure. Isn't that what love is all about? You sure you can carry that all the way back?"

"I think I can manage. I've done it before."

"That you have, lass. That you have. Theresa!" he called. "If you be feeling lonely, give a jingle!"

"I will."

That night the rain came back, not in a gale, but softly. Theresa popped some corn, drank diet soda and worked late on her book. It was a way not to think.

Another way not to think was to listen to the mice. The babies' eyes were open now and they were growing, falling out of the pocket on a regular basis. She could often hear their little squeaks and scampers behind the bathroom door. Hungry little baby mice were one thing, but growing mice? That scampered about? She went into the bathroom only when she had to, and she was tempted to put them all outside and plug up the hole. But not tonight. Maybe in the morning.

But in the morning it was still raining, a light rain— sugar mist, they called it in Seattle. She didn't have the heart to oust them from the warm nest. She'd wait until it was sunny.

175

For her Bible reading she turned back to Jeremiah 29:11. "For I know the plans I have for you . . . to give you a future and a hope."

Boy, I sure bungled that one, she thought. What a glorious future it could have been—if she hadn't been so blind. She thought of Shawn and bit her lip. Had he gone home, wherever that was? Was he just out sailing? Where was he? What was he thinking? And what did he think of her?

She dressed warmly, putting on the sailboat sweatshirt, laundered since the last time she'd worn it—the day Shawn had been here and they had—

Stop it, she told herself. She pulled on her wool socks.

She'd only been typing a short time, was in the middle of page 101, when she heard a short holler. It came again. Someone was hollering down on the beach! Throwing on her jacket, tossing aside junk until she found her gum boots buried in a corner by the water heater, and tore out of the cabin, taking the steps two at a time. Maybe someone was drowning. At the top of the cliff she stopped and scanned the beach. The tide was halfway in, nudging seaweed ropes closer to the cliff.

"Theresa!"

She whirled. The voice wasn't coming from the beach at all, but from behind the cabin.

"Shawn!" There he was, coming through the grass. *If a body meet a body, coming through the rye.* He was whistling in the rain, grinning, walking fast.

"Shawn!" she screamed, and then they were both running, flying over stumps and brush and raccoon holes. And then she was in his arms, crying and laughing and reaching for his kisses and listening to him say, "I love you," over and over and over.

"Oh, Shawn!" she cried. She hardly knew what else to say, except that she knew everything was all right now. How and why, she didn't know. She didn't care. He was here, loving her. He picked her up and carried her into the cabin, kicked the door shut, then stood her against the wall where he kissed her long and slow, and more passionately than she had ever been kissed in her life.

"You silly goose," he finally said, drawing back, taking a deep breath. "You silly, silly goose."

"Oh, Shawn, I'm so sorry. Please let me explain."

He stopped her with a kiss. "Shh. I just saw Mr. McCullough. He explained the whole thing."

She put her forehead against his chest and hung onto the wet opening of his jacket, too embarrassed to look up.

He kissed the top of her head. "I was on my way back to you—but thought I'd pick up some more lemon cheese, or some all-sorts—something special before I came out. And Mr. McCullough told me—"

"You were on your way to see me?" she asked quietly, staring down at the floor. His chest was warm against her forehead.

"Right. I finished my research, and was coming back as I promised." His hand slid beneath her chin and forced her head up. "You mean to say you figured I wouldn't come back?"

"But—"

"Don't you remember that I promised? I couldn't break a promise. Besides what would that do to your sense of abandonment and all?"

"But I was the one who abandoned you! With no explanation, no—"

Hurt flickered through his eyes. "That *was* a bit of a

surprise. To find you gone. But you ought to have known that that wouldn't stop me from coming back to see you. I was upset, yes. Angry, too, I think. But a promise is a promise." The hurt passed and the old mischief danced in. "I *had* to come back—at least long enough to rattle a reason for such unruly behavior out of you!"

"I thought—"

"Shh! Mr. McCullough supplied all the explanations that are necessary. Let's not talk about it. Other than to say that *if* and *when* I go for a real job—it'll be with Young Life, I expect. But my writing is what I'm called to do, at least for now." He shook his head suddenly and put his hands on her shoulders, pinning her to the wall. "You and I are going to write. I love you, you silly, silly goose."

He looked wonderful. Red in his cheeks, hair all messed up and wet, so alive and real, all excited and breathless, his head just clearing the ceiling.

"Oh, Shawn, I should have waited for you! I . . ." She started pulling on her jacket zipper nervously, yanking it down in little jabs as tears threatened to flow.

"Hey, don't do that," he said, pulling her into him and engulfing her in his arms. "And why are you crying?"

"I can't get my jacket zipped."

He pulled out his bandana, and while she wiped her eyes he zipped up her jacket—to the chin.

"Where are we going?"

"I want to go outside for a bit before we dry off. Okay?"

"In this weather?"

"We've been out in worse."

That was true.

"I want to go climb back up on that boulder again."

She didn't even ask why. She just followed him out the door, down to the beach, and up the rock. Today she'd do anything he asked.

"Where's your boat?"

"At the marina. Don't know what this weather is going to do. Actually," he said, looking overhead, "I think it might clear up. The clouds. . . . But you don't want a weather lesson, do you?" He laughed, pulling her close to him as he sat on the very top of the rock. The rock was ice cold and she shivered, but his arms were warm.

"No. Where's Bear?"

"I left him with Mr. McCullough."

She almost laughed. "Mr. McCullough! How on earth did you talk *him* into babysitting your dog?"

"Because I told him I had a very important mission to accomplish. Don't you want to know why I wanted to come back out here, on this wet rock?"

He was here, he was really here. He had come back. And Mr. McCullough was right. Shawn had come back because he loved her.

"Remember the last time we were out here?" he persisted.

"It was in the rain."

"Getting drenched to the bone. I wanted to do something then, but I didn't." He turned her face to meet his, and his eyes were warm and loving. "I want to do it now."

"What's that?" she asked breathlessly.

"I want to ask you to marry me."

Marry?

The waves rolled over the boulder, gray waves,

rolling and breaking and washing out. "Will you marry me, Theresa?" he asked again.

"Oh, Shawn, why do you want to marry *me?*"

"Because I love you."

"But I don't deserve you!"

He stopped her with a kiss. The sugar mist moistened her closed eyes while he tilted her head, trailing a row of small, wet kisses down her throat, whispering, "I love you, I love you," between each one.

"Please say yes," he whispered, coming back to her mouth.

"I shouldn't have left you. I shouldn't have—"

He took her face in his hands and looked into her eyes. "Theresa don't you know that I love you?"

"I do."

"Then marry me," he murmured. "Let's live the rest of our lives writing and working for God. He brought us together, you know."

She had no doubt that it was true. And as she looked up into Shawn's eyes—his wonderful, deep brown eyes—she knew that God was in heaven and all was well with the world. "Yes, Shawn, I'll marry you."

Only gradually was she aware that the mist was gone. The sun, a weak yellow, screened behind the low gray clouds, was directly overhead. The gray broke and pale blue hung over them. Shawn kissed her cheeks. "You're crying again."

"Maybe because I'm so happy."

"I don't want to see you cry anymore," he whispered, rubbing her tears away, pushing his nose into her hair. "You've cried enough."

"But these are tears of joy. Oh, Shawn, look!"

Glowing out of the pale blue was a rainbow, spilling from heaven to just behind the cabin up on the bluff.

"It's another promise," she whispered, slipping her arms around his neck.

"And what's that?" he asked, folding her in his arms.

"That God collects *all* our tears—unhappy tears, and the joyful tears."

The rainbow grew bright as the sun shone through.

"It looks as though the pot of gold might be behind the shed," she whispered.

"Should we go find it?" he whispered back.

"I think we've already found it."

He bent over her, and she knew that they had.

ABOUT THE AUTHOR

The award-winning author of historical and contemporary romance novels, BRENDA WILLOUGHBY is a full time writer, lecturer, and speaker. She writes for national magazines, and her three books sell internationally. Brenda teaches at writers' conferences. She conducts her own creative writing seminars through the University of Washington. And as Founder / Director of the Literary Service Agency of Seattle, she acts as editor and consultant in the Pacific Northwest. Her most recent project is *The Author's Taxi*, a facilitating service for "on-tour" authors.

Brenda is the single "mum" of three small children, Heather, Phillip, and Blake. They feel lucky to have a mom that writes "because we get to be in her books!" Mum says, "Feather, Mr. Flip, and Cornblake are in the works. That's the *next* book."

A Letter to Our Readers

Dear Reader:

Welcome to the world of Serenade Books—a series designed to bring you the most beautiful love stories in the world of inspirational romance. They will uplift you, encourage you, and provide hours of wholesome entertainment, so thousands of readers have testified. In order that we might better contribute to your reading enjoyment, we would appreciate your taking a few minutes to respond to the following questions and return to:

> Editor, Serenade Books
> The Zondervan Publishing House
> 1415 Lake Drive, S.E.
> Grand Rapids, Michigan 49506

1. Did you enjoy reading THETIS ISLAND?

   ☐ Very much. I would like to see more books by this author!
   ☐ Moderately
   ☐ I would have enjoyed it more if _____

   _____

2. Where did you purchase this book? _____

3. What influenced your decision to purchase this book?

   ☐ Cover   ☐ Back cover copy
   ☐ Title   ☐ Friends
   ☐ Publicity   ☐ Other _____

183

4. What are some inspirational themes you would like to see treated in future books?

_____

5. Please indicate your age range:

☐ Under 18   ☐ 25–34   ☐ 46–55
☐ 18–24   ☐ 35–45   ☐ Over 55

6. If you are interested in receiving information about our Serenade Home Reader Service, in which you will be offered new and exciting novels on a regular basis, please give us your name and address. (This does NOT obligate you for membership.)

Name _____

Occupation _____

Address _____

City _____ State _____ Zip _____

Serenade / Saga books are inspirational romances in historical settings, designed to bring you a joyful, heart-lifting reading experience.

Serenade / Saga books available in your local book store:

Serenade / Serenata books are inspirational romances in contemporary settings, designed to bring you a joyful, heart-lifting reading experience.

Serenade / Serenata books available in your local bookstore:

Watch for other books in both the *Serenade/Saga* (historical) and *Serenade/Serenata* (contemporary) series coming soon.